AFTER THE RAIN

Peacock Publishing Ltd

Peacock MYSTERIES OF THE HEART

1997

After the Rain

Published by Peacock Publishing Ltd
3, St. Mary's Street
Worcester WR1 1HA, England

ISBN 0-9525404-7-9

Cover design: Excalibur Graphics 1997

British Library cataloguing-in-print data has been applied for

Typeset in Century Schoolbook 10.5pt

Printed in Malta by Interprint Ltd

CHAPTER 1

I just had to stop. I'd never have believed working for Ralph could be so exhausting. I'd tried my best to refuse his offer in the first place because I had a feeling that, once I started, I'd end up facing a dead-end job for the rest of my life and never experience any of the excitement I'd always longed for.

So, after one morning in Ralph's bookshop, I felt I'd had enough. Outside in the street, I could see the wet, shiny road crowded with traffic and heedless pedestrians nipping in and out of the cars, just missing their bumpers and ignoring the looks of all the frustrated motorists.

Working in a second-hand bookshop on a wet, Saturday morning in London wasn't quite my idea of an exciting life. On account of the rain, the shop was full of people looking for bargains, pulling out the books, reading them on the spot and asking me questions I couldn't answer.

Besides, I wasn't a real bookseller like Ralph, who specialised in military history. I felt a flutter of panic each time I was approached with a request for some obscure title. Each time I had to find my cousin to help me, the customer was plainly thinking, well, she doesn't know much. What's she paid for?

It wasn't that I didn't like books - I did - it was just that I'd imagined myself doing something so different, like being in the midst of things, or driving a car like the black Porsche which had just managed to squeeze miraculously into the tiniest space outside the shop window.

I didn't have time to see the driver and I didn't want to. After what had happened to me, I knew there wasn't much chance of me ever driving a sports again. My own car, a nippy Escort, was safe in the garage and I took either the bus or the Underground every morning.

I turned to look for Ralph because I sensed the tubby women in the silk headscarf was going to ask me something I didn't know and should have done. At least it couldn't be military history this time. She'd been poking around for ages in the cookery section, and here she was, thrusting three books at me.

"Have you the other?" she queried.

"The other?"

The women was glaring at me as if I were a simpleton.

"These are the first three in the series." Her tone was fairly nasty. "Have you the fourth?"

"I'll just go and look."

I was stalling, and hurried round the counter towards the back of the shop in search of Ralph. He was shelving a pile of hardbacks, examining each one meticulously.

Ralph was everyone's idea of a second-hand bookseller: green, floppy, lambswool cardigan pulled straight down over grey, flannel trousers; thick-rimmed glasses through which he peered endlessly, and with a bald spot which gleamed

"Just a minute, Alison, just a minute."

He seemed to have all the time in the world. What a way to run a business.

"Have we the other of these?" I asked hopefully, holding a volume up to him.

His expert eye was already summing up the series as he nodded.

"Yes. They're in the back."

"Where?" I grimaced. "Where do I look?"

"Just a minute. Just a minute," he repeated. "You'll have to learn to calm down a bit Alison, if you're going to survive. We can't do everything at once."

"Yes, Ralph."

I sighed, remembering that this wasn't Knightsbridge or Regent Street, but a nondescript, little shop on Shaftesbury Avenue, owned by my learned cousin and full of ordinary people on the look-out for the best bargains they could find.

Ralph got up from his knees with a grunt, took another look at the book I was holding and disappeared into the back room. I turned and squeezed hurriedly past the two students who were taking down notes secretly from several books on the History shelves.

"Sorry to keep you," I said to the customer I'd left. "He's just gone to fetch it."

She ignored me rather rudely and went on reading. I felt foolish for hurrying on her behalf, and a bit angry as well. Maybe there was something in what cousin Ralph said. I couldn't do everything on the double.

Wanting to get on with the job had always been my downfall. I'd always been too quick at everything - at summing up people, judging them and falling in love. If I hadn't fallen for Martin, I wouldn't be here now.

I stared miserably out of the window in the direction of Trafalgar Square. It would be the same down there as it always was - tourists and pigeons - the air full of whirring wings, drifting spray from the fountains, wet pavements under your feet. There would be thousands of people trooping in and out of the National Gallery just because it was a wet Saturday in summer.

I remembered a time when I enjoyed all those things, but that was history. It was probably the sports car in front of the window that had reminded me. I'd been really excited when I'd found a bloke who drove a car like that. Martin had meant a good time. He'd stood for excitement. . .

* * *

My love affair with the service started the day I sauntered about outside the Army careers office window. I'd always fancied an exciting life and the pictures of purposeful-eyed soldiers in camouflage staring out at me through the glass gave me a thrill.

Of course, I wasn't naive enough to believe it would be all roses. When you joined the Army you stood the chance of being killed and I didn't want that. But, at nearly eighteen, it seemed an extremely remote possibility.

The chap sitting at the desk inside looked up at me and smiled encouragingly. I hesitated thinking of what my mother would say. I was expecting to do well in my 'A Levels' and she and Dad had set their heart on me going to university and doing something *nice* with my life. That was their word, but the last thing I wanted to do was be stuck in some office. I'd always liked the outdoor life.

In fact, I'd resisted the idea so much that I hadn't even applied for a university place to do my degree. I intended to take a gap year instead and earn some money. The chap was still looking so I smiled back at him and pushed open the heavy glass door. . .

I remembered the look of utter amazement on my mother's face when I told her I intended to join the Army as an officer on a short service commission. She was horrified. "Whatever for, Alison? I can't believe it. It's a man's job." I wasn't prepared to take that. I believed a woman could do just as good as a man at anything. I'd show Mother.

"No, it isn't. There are lots of jobs for women in the Army. Imagine, if I do okay, I'll be in *charge* of men. A battalion." My father just looked at me. I knew he was thinking about his *little girl* leading a battalion of squaddies. But I could do it, I knew I could. As long as I could get through the selection process and into Sandhurst. It wasn't going to be easy.

But Mum kept going on and on, "I'm sure you'd like to do a degree instead. What about your Biology? You're so good at it. Couldn't you take that up?"

9

But I wouldn't listen.

Later, I remembered her words and wondered what Mum would make of the biology I learned in the Army - and especially from Martin. At that time I didn't have a real boyfriend. I expect I was looking for a *real* man - and I was sure I'd find plenty of those very soon.

When Mum found out just how difficult it was to get into Sandhurst, she was beginning to come round. In fact, she was soon telling all her friends how proud she was of me. And I knew Dad was - he'd been a Commando himself and was for ever joking the Army was a soft option these days.

But, in the end, they'd both come round and at the passing-out parade, they were grinning like the rest of the parents. I think that, after all the opposition, Mum and Dad thought being an Army officer today was quite a glamorous career, that's if you discounted a tour in Northern Ireland. I made a point of not telling Mum about the mud, the punishing exercises and all the jokes.

In spite of the latter, the Army became to be everything I'd ever dreamed of and even more so, when Martin and I finally got ourselves together. . .

Three years later, I could see that was my first mistake but, in those few seconds of memory, I'd been speeding away from Ralph's little shop and musty, ancient books, driving open-topped to new and secret places, overnight bags in the back, with the car responding to our excitement, accelerating away from Shaftesbury Avenue, through the traffic lanes and down to the M4 motorway, never thinking of danger. . .

It hadn't paid off, though, falling in love with Martin. I rubbed my leg instinctively; something I always did when it felt tired and useless. Why did I have to fall for Martin, the bright, young cadet with more money than sense? The first time we'd really spoken had done it. He was public school through and through, and said he hadn't particularly wanted to go into the Army, but all the men in his family did. It was a tradition he told me.

"Well," I said, "you still didn't have to, Martin. Tradition's OK. None of us would be here if it wasn't. But if you feel you don't fit in. . ."

It was the only time I had seen him serious when he replied. "I have to. There's been one of us in the Army since Waterloo."

I thought I wasn't impressed but there was a lump in my throat. However, I believed in reality.

"What else would you have done, if you hadn't?"

I remembered too, the Sunday I'd said it, that first exercise when we were staked out on Salisbury Plain, getting a few minutes outside the tent we'd set up.

"Not much, except drive fast cars. I'd have made a brilliant racing driver."

That really surprised me, not because I couldn't imagine him doing it but because he really was cut out to be an officer. He had the talent for it and all the qualities of leadership. He was a sportsman, too. In fact, he was good at everything, and extremely good-looking.

"What else do you like doing?" I'd continued, squinting against the sun, which was making his face a shadowy blur.

"Going out with girls who don't ask too many questions."

Then he walked away quite deliberately and left me to talk to someone else.

After that, landing Martin was just another challenge. I wanted to know what made him tick, why he had such a chip in his shoulder. I suppose I chased him. That did occur to me when he became colder and more distant. But that was still in the future. . .

We met again later that day as we were eating our evening meal. We had more time to talk on exercise instead of when we were at base. There, we were on the run all the time, almost standing up to eat. It was supposed to instil discipline, but it gave me indigestion. There was hardly ever time to talk personally.

But, tonight, we were sitting in our tent in a small group of four. Two lads and two girls. Tara, my friend, gave me a funny old-fashioned look when she saw that Martin and I were getting on so well. I didn't know why.

In fact, looking back I hardly knew anything. I should have checked, but it was exciting being singled out by the best-looking cadet in the year.

I'd never thought myself particularly pretty, although I made up for it by being brainy and efficient. I told myself that, anyway. Tara and the other lad were involved in a conversation too and, a few minutes later, I was watching them getting up and going outside. That left me with Martin.

"Well, I suppose we've a few minutes to relax," I said. He was looking at me with those fascinating eyes, which made my heart thud a little bit too fast.

12

"Great. So what shall we talk about?" He had a beautiful accent.

"Work?"

"Oh, please!" he begged sarcastically. "No thank you. You know, I should have got to know you before..."

"Before what?" I asked.

"Just before."

"You mean, you never noticed me," I replied, regretting the remark immediately.

"Oh, I did, but I never got round to talking to you. As you said, our life's about work. I think it's a plot on the part of the Army."

"What is?"

"Keeping the blokes and the girls apart."

"I hope not," I retorted, really meaning it.

"Under its skin, the Army is still terribly old-fashioned," he stated. "It pretends to be modern but, in there," Martin tapped his shirt and the place where his heart was, "it has always been the same. Traditional. Look at the rules, for instance."

"For instance?"

"Having to leave the service if a girl gets pregnant." I hadn't been expecting him to say that and suddenly, I felt very hot in my camouflage. Those eyes were regarding me wickedly.

"Oh, and you'd know about that, would you?" I quipped. "Well, we can't have women officers getting pregnant, can we?" My attempt at sarcasm was poor.

"Actually, getting pregnant can be a hell of a lot of fun." He laughed out loud.

I knew my face had gone red and I was ashamed of it. I never blushed and why on earth should I with

13

him? But I didn't really like what he'd said. It was a bit too soon for me. "Don't you think you ought to be going now?" I asked, looking at my watch and wondering what had happened to Tara and the other bloke.

"Is that a hint?"

My heart was thudding. He was so close and I could feel it through the whole of my body. . .

Just then, Tara stuck her head through the tent flap. "Come on, you two. The CO's expecting us for a briefing about tomorrow morning."

I saw Martin's face. He was as disappointed as I was. At that moment, I knew I wanted more and more risky conversations with him.

And I got my chance.

I soon learned that Martin was disenchanted with Army life. I never asked him again why he joined because it was quite obvious. He had done it because it was expected of him. It had always been pointed out to him as the only career even from a little boy. He knew he had to be an officer. And he was so good at it.

Time and time again I thought what a waste it was that his heart wasn't really in it. I wondered too how the selection board hadn't found it out. But Martin had excellent connections.

And all the time, we were getting closer and closer. When we had a few minutes off, we used to come and find each other in the bar or wherever. We'd talk about the strangest things. Well, I'd talk. He hardly ever said anything about his past or his family, but Tara had let a few things slip. . .

He took me to Silverstone on our first date. I didn't know anything about motor racing, but he knew everything and everyone. I looked at the car he was proposing to drive round the circuit. I don't know whether fear showed in my face, but Martin was quick to pick it up.

He grinned, his clear-cut striking features so like those pictures which had first attracted me to the Army. I could see him facing everything and I wondered if his ancestor had looked like that fighting the French at Waterloo.

Martin had blue, blue eyes which pierced through you from under blond eyelashes like a girl's. But there was nothing girlish about him. His hair flopped fashionably over his eyes as he looked away from me and down at the vehicle.

I couldn't believe it. I'd never seen anything like it and he wanted me to get in. That was why he'd insisted I wear the overalls and helmet. I stared back at him, then at the car. He was looking too and in that moment I knew where his real allegiance lay.

"It's a Lola," he said. "T592."

I'd never heard of the car but it was as low and sleek as a stealth bomber. Black. Sinister. Heart-turning.

"Well, are you just going to stand there, Ally?"

"It's . . ." I didn't know how to describe it. He did.

"It's got everything. And can it go. Come on, Ally, it's the chance of a lifetime."

"How often do you do this?" I asked as the bodywork opened up. He didn't answer. There were no doors; you had to step in over the side. "But there isn't a seat," I protested. There was just an empty space in the aluminium tub of a body.

He was standing waiting round the other side. "I can get one put in for you if you like - but it'll be fun without it. See, you can hold on here." He pointed to the roll bar. "You'll be okay - that's if you can stand it."

"Is this a test?" I replied coolly as I stepped over into the Lola. Inside, my heartbeat was accelerating but, outside, I was calm. I was an officer in HM Forces and I gave as good as I got.

"So you're not scared then?" There was a hint of admiration in his voice.

"What do you think?" I retorted and squeezed myself into the power machine.

And that was when Martin came really alive - when he had an engine like that to taunt and caress. He fastened my six-point harness and his own. It was then I realised there was no windscreen. The body work was just wrapped round the engine at the back.

I glanced at his hands stroking the tiny three-spoked steering wheel which couldn't have been more than 20 centimetres in diameter. He was shouting something at me as he started up. It sounded like, "You'll find it different from my Porsche."

There was something in me that thrilled to the speed although I was frightened to death. The sound of the engine was horrendous and the ride was white knuckle all the way.

What he'd said abut wanting to be a racing driver was perfectly obvious. Martin had it in him; he appeared to be revelling in every mad thrust and turn, and what I had thought then was wonderful and brave, looking back now seemed to me to be reckless and foolish.

On that first lap of the circuit, we almost flew. Several times I darted a glance at him but he was entirely oblivious of anything but speed. As the track surface spread in front of us, I thought we were going to take off. Once or twice, I gritted my teeth to stop crying out as he took the car up to over 100mph, but he was a brilliant driver and I thought I loved him.

I could hardly stand up when I got out, but I didn't want to show it. And the smell of the Lola's burning hot body was filling my nostrils, like the sweet cloying scent of a warm Crunchie bar.

He took my arm because my legs were wobbling like mad. I looked down at my ankles and boots which were covered with tiny bits of rubber.

"That's part of the tyres," he grinned.

"What?"

"Don't worry. We were quite safe. It takes two circuits anyway to warm them up. The bits come through little apertures in the bodywork. . ."

Then I had it all, every little detail of his beloved Lola. But I didn't care. When he talked about cars Martin came alive - and I liked that. It seemed like they were the only things that could give him a real buzz - except me, of course.

We had our first night together at a small exclusive hotel not far from the circuit. It should have been everything else I dreamed of but, as we snuggled together in bed, I suddenly thought that if ever Martin asked me to marry him he'd probably want me to leave the Army and stay at home on that country estate of his, keeping watch over his beloved classic cars.

We certainly couldn't live together if we were both Army officers. And word would get round. It always did. The Army didn't like its men and women living in sin. And, anyway, I had my career to consider.

He opened his arms and I was next to his silky skin, my head nuzzling his chest. Then he was turning his face to me and kissing my lips. . . But Martin never said he loved me. Ever. Mind you, I didn't expect it at first, but I began to afterwards. And it still didn't come.

After we became lovers, things started to happen, and I began to understand at last why Martin was like he was and why, finally, he did what he did. . .

* * *

CHAPTER 2

Martin and I were on an exercise in the Black Mountains and trying to avoid each other. I know that a couple of my closest friends realised things were happening between us.

At first, I thought the hostility my special friend, Tara, showed towards Martin was based on jealousy. I don't know how I could have, as Tara was the least jealous person I've ever met. But she wasn't seeing anybody and what girl could help being attracted to the devastatingly handsome and devil-may-care Martin. I was feeling mean when I said so.

We'd just stolen a quick - and what we thought secret - kiss in between the tents on one of our many exercises. There was no time for that sort of thing on duty, and our commanding officer would have gone mad if he'd known. I suppose I wasn't thinking about weakness creeping into our professional thinking, but it was Tara who pointed it out, and I accused her.

"You're only jealous," I said.

"What?" She could hardly believe her ears. A blush rose right up to her ears, making her fine porcelain skin red.

"Nobody saw," I added scathingly.

"Well, I did," she replied, "and, seriously, you and Martin ought to be careful. You'll get in trouble if you're caught"

"There's no law against kissing your boy friend," I replied nastily.

"No, but I'd call it unwise. Not illegal. And so would the colonel. He hates messing about like that. Anyway, if you and Martin are so stuck on each other perhaps you shouldn't both be here."

"You're a prude, Tara," I said hotly. "Neither Martin nor I are jeopardising anything on this exercise. We're just in love."

"Are you?" she said. "And, remember, Ally, I'm your friend. Just watch out, that's all. Martin's a very strange guy." Then Tara turned and walked away, her blonde hair glinting in the sun.

I went over what she said a million times on that exercise, and I wondered too if she'd mentioned anything to Martin because, for the rest of the time, we never went near each other personally, and he offered not the slightest explanation.

I thought even more about it when we were scaling an extremely large mountain in Wales. It had started to rain, the wind was vile and I never thought I'd reach the top.

Martin, as usual, was getting up faster than anyone else. He was roped in with another couple of cadets and making them keep up with the pace. It was a good thing they were up to it or the three of them might have fallen.

When, finally, I got to the top, the other two boys

20

were lying on the ground, breathing heavily, their faces streaked with grime and sweat. Martin was sitting coolly on the edge of the drop, grinning. His face was streaming wet, washed pale but he looked, as usual, in full control. There was nothing to show of the effort he'd put into that crazy climb; that battle against the wind and the rain.

But, as I heaved myself past him, I could see something else in his eyes - contempt for the rest of us who hadn't got what he had. It hit me suddenly. Why the hell did he always have to better than anyone else? What was he trying to prove? And I couldn't say a word to him. There was no opportunity. There never would be.

I should have been proud of him then, but I wasn't. Only angry - in case he'd hurt himself and them. I knew afterwards that our commanding officer had had words with him. I could imagine what he'd said, but Martin never breathed a word. He was used to it. And then I thought of all the times I'd seen him do the same things.

Lots of the team said he'd win the sword as the best cadet. But I wasn't surprised when he didn't. Sometimes, it looked like he had some bizarre death wish. I wish I'd taken notice of my instincts.

He even took me home to meet his parents. That was an ordeal. He's spoken about home often enough and when he did it gave me both shivers of fear and excitement. Somehow, I didn't think I was going to fit into the social scene.

"You're not afraid of my parents?" he'd challenged.

"Well, it's going to be first time for me," I replied.

21

"What is?" He was stroking my hair at the time.

"Meeting a general."

"Oh, the old man's okay. I know how to get round him. And so's the mater."

I made a face at the public-school term. I could hardly believe anyone used such words any more. But I knew why when I met her. She was cold. I couldn't imagine her loving anyone. She was perfectly polite to me but, all the time, I knew she was thinking I wasn't good enough for her son. She almost said so, but was far too well-bred to carry on. However, she intimated I wasn't the only girl Martin had brought home. . .

"Is it true?" I asked as we walked through their lovely conservatory, crammed full of orchids. I was thinking about Dad's little greenhouse at the time.

"Is what true?"

"What Mummy said. You've been out with lots of women? Brought them here?"

"For heaven's sake, Ally. Are you jealous?"

"I don't know," I said, staring at the sad face of an extremely beautiful orchid.

"I bet you are," grinned Martin, taking me in his arms. "That's good. And, anyway, I didn't like them as much as you. You've got more nerve. They were wimps."

"So - where did you meet them?" I persisted.

"At school."

"At school," I repeated. "How old were you then?"

"Old enough. Blokes I knew. Their sisters mostly. . . Here . . ." he looked around the conservatory and out of the window across the rolling lawn. He grimaced, "I'm expected to meet that kind of girl. . ."

"You mean the kind your mother wants you to marry; the right kind who'd fit in." I couldn't help stating the obvious.

"Who said anything about *marry*?" And there was a tone to Martin's voice I'd never heard before. "I shall never marry."

I couldn't say a word, but my heart jumped about inside my chest. What were we doing then? The two of us. Was there to be no future for Martin nor me?

Afterwards, I believed his remark had been an omen. But then, although in a way I was glad because of my career, I was horribly disappointed too. Martin had said he wasn't going to marry anyone - and I had realised instinctively what he'd said to me that afternoon at his parents' home was absolutely true.

Our passing-out parade that year was something of a surprise. As I said, Martin didn't get the sword, but Tara did. I knew she was a career soldier like me and that she was good at most things but, somehow, I hadn't thought it would be her.

We'd remained friends in spite of the fact she didn't approve of Martin. I found out why later. But at the parade I was feeling a bit put-out. I wasn't jealous of her, but I had to admit she'd had all the advantages. She was officer material, like Martin, and her father was a brigadier. There was gleaming pride in his eyes when she introduced me to him.

My parents seemed totally overawed with all the spit and polish, and even the old Commando in my father seemed satisfied.

When my parents and hers were talking, we got the chance to be alone. I can't recall where Martin was at the time, but looking into Tara's sparkling eyes made me feel really happy.

I squeezed her hand. "I'm so proud of you," I said, "and by the look of it, so is everyone else."

She glanced across in the direction of her father. "Thanks," she said. "Well, I just had to do it, didn't I? Or he'd have given me a dog's life." We both laughed. "Were you disappointed Martin didn't get the sword?" she asked, looking me straight in the eye.

"No, not really and, anyway, I didn't think he would."

"You didn't?"

"No, Tara, he's not that dedicated, really. I shouldn't say it, but it's true. Not like us. He comes from the right background but, you know, sometimes I think he hates the Army." Tara looked extremely startled and I swivelled my eyes just in case anyone had heard me.

"What makes you say that, Ally?" Tara's voice sounded flat and troubled.

"Well, he's always trying to prove he's the best at everything and he can't always be. I know that. And it isn't healthy."

"Well, well," said Tara, smiling. "How long did it take for you to figure that out?"

"Too long. But it doesn't mean I don't care for him," I flashed.

Tara sighed. "I know you do, Ally, but be careful, won't you. He might break your heart."

"What do you mean?"

"Nothing - except - I've known Martin for a long time."

24

"You never said."

"Well, I didn't want to upset you, Ally. He and I grew up together actually. Generals and brigadiers." She smiled ruefully. "He was always like that, even when he was a little boy. He broke everything."

I grinned. I couldn't help it, thinking what a little devil he must have been. "Not on purpose surely?"

"Maybe. But my brother said he was the same at Shrewsbury. He was popular - fantastic at sports - but really wild. As though there was something mad inside, something that wanted to come out. As if he had it in for everyone and everybody."

"His mother probably made him like that," I said, thinking about her.

"Probably but, sometimes, Ally, when I see the two of you together, I just get the shivers. You're both so cool and in control. But which one of you'll get the upper hand?" I didn't like the expression on Tara's face.

"Neither, hopefully. It'll be a partnership." It was an extremely good lie.

"Well, I hope so, for your sake," replied Tara, smiling at our parents who were coming over. As they did, she whispered, "Have you thought how you'll manage when you're married to him?"

I shook my head. It was nice pretending, but it'd never happen. But I wasn't going to let Tara know.

Later, as Martin stood chatting to my parents, I wondered how Mum would feel if I married him. I could see by her face she was as stuck on him as every woman he was nice to, whatever age. Yes, Martin was charming, but I knew when he reserved the best for me, I had to pay for it. By now I thought it couldn't be love between us, but some monstrous, self-destroying attraction and desire, which ate us up, and one day would spit us out, just as easily. . .

I remember that week when we got our postings. Martin was waiting for me in the hall. I was flushed with happiness. In fact, I'd almost forgotten all about where he might be sent. I was thrilled. I was being sent to Germany and, what's more, there were only two other women on the base. I wondered what Dad was going to say about that.

"Germany!" I said. "Gosh, Martin, I can't believe it! Sub-Lieutenant Dean is on her way up at last. What about you?" All of a sudden, I was a bit afraid of what I was going to do without the thrill of Martin in my life.

Somewhere, inside, I'd had my speech prepared for ages. I was sure he couldn't do without me either, because I was the perfect foil. I went along with everything and took it as well as he did. He'd never find another girl like me. If he did finally ask me to marry him, I'd have to say *no* for the present, but certainly *sometime*. Instead, his reaction was surprising.

"That's it then," he said.

"What do you mean, Martin?" My legs were trembling.

"I mean you get Germany and I get rotten, boring London."

"What?"

"My father's old regiment, of course. Guard duty etc. Ceremonial and all that trash." His eyes had a fanatical light in them.

"Well, can't you protest?" It was something to say as I knew he couldn't.

"I asked for it, didn't I?"

"You mean you chose your posting?" I couldn't believe what he was saying.

"Tradition, darling. That old chestnut. Daddy's brigade and all that. Palace duty. I was groomed for it." I tried to avoid the hard look in those bright blue eyes. But Martin caught hold of my hand and squeezed until it hurt. "It's goodbye to Action Man now, Ally."

"Why? I'll be back, won't I? And there's the phone. We get leave, and the world's shrinking all the time, Martin."

"Rubbish." He was so angry it was frightening, and it was nothing to do with me. I watched him walk off in a huff, and what should have been a really happy day had turned into a nightmare. . . Suddenly, I was questioning what kind of an officer Martin would make after all. And I knew by then I wouldn't make an officer's wife.

Next weekend I was driving down to his Huntingdon home. He'd been adamant on the phone. He had to see me, he said. He was sorry how he'd behaved. It was nothing to do with me. It was just because he was upset.

As I drove through the lanes in my smart new XR3i, I was thinking his wasn't a bad posting at all. London was fine. And he'd be able to drive the Porsche all the time, and the classic Aston Martin in his father's garage. And he could still go for test days at Silverstone. Cushy really.

As I accelerated, I concluded I liked speed nearly

as much as Martin did, but I didn't have quite as much nerve. But he'd never find out. As I streaked up the long drive to his house I thought for the hundredth time that Martin was a lucky bloke to have all he had. As Tara had said, his parents had spoiled him rotten.

Then I thought more about Tara, what she'd told me after my quarrel with Martin. She had been one of those "sisters of his friends". And she said she had to tell me things about his past, even though I probably didn't want to listen. And I didn't.

Maybe, inside, I still suspected she was jealous of our relationship? She had said it was because she was afraid I might marry him. I had had no intention of letting her know what he'd said to me earlier. Perhaps he'd change when he grew up a bit? And then, well, who knows?

Tara and Martin had hardly exchanged a word all the time at Sandhurst except when they had to? She'd explained why, and I'd listened, hardly taking it in. What she'd told me about him had been a long time ago. It couldn't happen again. Martin's past emotional life was a puzzle I didn't feel able to unravel.

As I said before, Martin's house was wonderful. As well as the marvellous hothouse and its orchids, there were stables and outhouses, even an exercise room in what had once been a dilapidated barn.

His mother seemed almost pleased to see me that day. Evidently, he'd been giving her a hard time too about his posting. She looked not quite as confident and beautifully groomed as usual.

"Hello, Alison. How are you?"

"Fine, thank you." I walked into the spacious hall. She was following and, suddenly, I could feel the atmosphere. I stood uncertainly as I was pretty sure Martin's mother didn't approve of his choice.

"I'm glad you've come," she said, surprising me. "Martin's in the gym. Oh, but before you go . . ." I looked down at the heavily-ringed hand on my arm, "I'd be happy if we could have a word." It seemed that Martin had been dreadfully quiet all the week. That once or twice, when either she or his dad had tried to ask what was the matter, he'd snapped at them and gone off by himself. I looked into her puffy eyes. She'd been crying. Perhaps things in this lovely house weren't perfect after all. Had never been.

"I'd be very happy if you could find out what's the matter," she said. "I know he was somewhat upset about the posting, but he did apply for it, you know."

"I know," but I didn't know anything really. I was just his girlfriend. He's talked of *being upset* on the telephone, but I wasn't going to tell his mother that. I smiled at her in the friendliest way I could. "I'll try and find out what's the matter," I promised, "but you know Martin. He keeps things to himself."

It was small comfort but she looked grateful. . . When I left her, I hadn't any idea how depressed Martin really was. . .

He didn't want to talk to me. Not to anyone. He seemed to be totally despondent. How many times since had I wished I'd known the signs? I sat by him in the exercise room. He hadn't been working out, just sitting there, looking at the apparatus - as if nothing mattered any more.

When I suggested going out in the car, he seemed to cheer up. I said it because I knew he loved driving and I thought it would take him out of himself. In fact, his eyes shone when I suggested it; but nothing else in his face seemed to have expression.

I didn't dare mention anything about the posting but, as we walked to the garage, I remarked, "Your mother seemed a bit worried about you, Martin." This evoked no response but I believed that if we went out for a drive and had lunch he might open up a bit.

Inside the garage we stood for a moment looking at the cars. His father hired a boy to wash and polish them - and he made a very good job of it. They were immaculate.

"The Porsche, I think," said Martin, jangling the keys.

"Sounds good," I joked.

But I was wrong and, from the very moment, he, and I roared off down the drive in the shiny black Porsche, which had had so much care lavished on it, I began to realise I'd made a big mistake. . .

When he shot the car into top gear, I'd glanced at him warily. He was driving much too fast, even for me. This wasn't a test around Silverstone; this was a country road - and it was beginning to rain. What had been a blinding hot summer's day was changing fast. It was extremely difficult to see anything through the windscreen, and how could he, if I couldn't?

Besides, we were so low on the road and the water in the gutters was rising over us like a cloud. We were in the middle of a heavy summer storm and Martin wasn't going to slow down. It was a horrible feeling.

Like what was about to happen was inevitable. I seemed to be freezing to the seat. I had not the slightest control over what was happening.

I shouted at him: "Martin. you're going too fast. Martin, please slow down. *Slow down.* I'm scared." It was the first time I'd ever said that. I was remembering the awful thing Tara had told me about him. I shouldn't have gone. And he didn't care. I could see it in his face and those mad, shining eyes fixed on the invisible road ahead.

"Please, please!" I screamed over the engine's noise and the splash of the water. "Please slow down, you'll kill us both!" I knew just how afraid I was as he turned to look at me. There was nothing recognisable about his face. He was looking right through me and his lips were moving like a robot. I couldn't believe what I heard.

"So what? I'd be glad. I hate the Army. I hate it. . ."

And those were the last words I ever heard him say. I remembered nothing more except noise, then darkness and, afterwards, my own voice screaming out in pain.

The rear end of the Porsche had stepped out - in layman's terms, the weight hangs over the rear wheels and, if pushed to the limit, there's always the possibility the car's back end will slide - especially in the rain - and catch you out, however brilliant a driver you are. And then you go off the road.

Funny, when I lay in hospital for all those weeks, I used to think about that boy who polished their cars. What did he say when he saw the mess Martin made of the sports?

So that's what happened to Martin and me. How I survived, I don't know, but I did. He didn't care, and he didn't. . .

In that one second, my memory had had me speeding away again from the little safe life I'd inflicted on myself. I used to blame Martin for the position I was in now but recently, more often than not, I blamed myself for not getting away from him when I knew the truth. But I'd been too stupid, too selfish, too set on a good time. . .

Once again, I rubbed my leg instinctively. I always did that when I was tired. There had been a pin in it for ages although no one would have guessed; the surgery was so good. I still felt like a bionic girl when I remembered what was holding my leg together. I remembered so vividly the surgeon's words when he told me I could go home after three months in hospital.

"And forget about fast cars."

It wasn't a very kind remark really, after what had happened to Martin, but I was nearly over it by then and, at least, I was alive.

I knew now I'd never loved him, only thought I had. In fact, our relationship had been over long before the accident. But, at least, he hadn't known that. It was going to be our last fling together. Ironic, considering he'd been flung from the car and died on the way to hospital. I suppose I was lucky that I never really loved him, or I would have never got over the accident.

There were so many things I would have done if I'd been fit, but the doctors said I had to take things easy, cut down on exercise until my leg settled down.

32

Would things ever settle down though? How was I going to face working in Ralph's shop after having to give up everything I ever loved - the exercise and the fun, the thrills of mountaineering - all those things a girl in the Army does as well as a man? Now Martin, the accident and my injured leg had cut down my options.

The chubby woman was beside me. While I'd been looking out of the window, thinking, Ralph had dropped Volume Four on the till desk. The woman was smiling in a peculiar way, half-satisfied and yet not at all.

"Thank you, dear, but they are rather expensive."

"You mean you don't want them?" I queried.

"No, not at this price. Do you think you could ask if you could get a bit knocked off for me?" She gave me a devious wink. "You know, a discount for the four?"

I winced as I came round again from behind the till. It was on a little dais and jarred my leg each time. Who had said this was going to be a sit down job? Once again, I pushed past the students towards Ralph.

"I'm sorry Ralph, but she wants to know if you'll give her any discount on those four books?"

"Dear me, Alison, I don't think so. What about my profit margin? And you shouldn't keep leaving the till. Don't worry." He must have seen the look on my face. "I'll come and sort it out."

I couldn't believe it when we got back to the counter. The woman had gone, and so had the books. I looked in horror at my cousin, and he stared at me.

"Lesson number one, Alison. Never trust the customer. He or she is hardly ever right."

"I'm so sorry, Ralph," I said.

"I know."

He patted my arm. He was a very nice man.

"Well, we'll never catch her now. It isn't worth the trouble." He sighed. "Working here takes a bit of getting used to and it'll take you some time. You get used to the fiddles. Come on, it isn't the end of the world. What about making us both a cup of coffee?

As I walked slowly back into the little, back room which served as both storeroom and kitchen, hot tears were stinging my eyes. How could the woman have stolen them? And how come I was crying over it? But they were tears of anger and frustration.

I'd had so much training to sharpen my senses. How could I have fallen for a trick like that? I knew then that, unless something else turned up soon, I was finished.

As I made the coffee, I tried to get things straight in my mind. Here I was, Alison Dean, formerly Sub-Lieutenant Dean, career over at twenty-one, cash in the bank and what was worst of all, plenty of time to spend it.

I did cry for Martin - a lot - but then I wasn't sure why. Now, I knew I'd been crying for myself as well as for him. I hated him, too, for what he'd done to me. I thought about his last words. It was so unfair, as the Army had meant so much to me.

"Alison Dean, drop-out," I whispered, half to myself. Then I realised I had poured the water on to the coffee and it was overflowing all over the work top in that tiny, back room. I jumped, put down the kettle and wiped up the mess. Then I mopped my nose with my hanky.

I sat down on the stool to recover. I looked round. It wasn't a bad little shop really. In spite of all my regrets, I found it quite interesting.

I used to keep glancing at the books I liked, especially the military history ones but, as soon as I picked one up, I had to drop it and attend to the till. I was probably the world's worst shop assistant. The thought made me smile. Ralph had been very good to put up with me, but wasn't he one of life's disasters as well?

He'd had a few bad experiences, losing his wife so early on in their marriage. My mother always referred to him as 'poor Ralph.' It sounded patronising but she didn't mean it. It was her way. But at least, he'd got himself together. Which was more than I could say. Mum had jumped at the chance when he'd suggested I worked for him for a while, until I got my life sorted out. I had to get back on my feet, too.

Sighing, I put three spoons of sugar in Ralph's cup. I could hear the rain pouring down the drainpipe outside and felt even gloomier. Picking up the cups, I carried the coffee through to the counter where Ralph was packing paperbacks for a queue of customers.

Standing by him, I sipped mine. When he'd finished, he looked at me over his spectacles.

"You're tired, aren't you? The old war wound?" Just like a man. He had no idea how the joke hurt, however kindly it was meant. "It's nearly lunchtime," he added. "Go and have a bite somewhere."

"What about you?"

"Oh, I've brought mine. I never go out at lunchtime."

"Thank you, Ralph. I won't be long."

"Pity it's raining," he said, jerking his head towards the window.

I limped a little as I fetched my raincoat. That worried me so I tried to straighten up like I used to when I was doing drill, but it was no good. I put on the trench-coat. It made me feel a little like I used to. My mother had bought me the Burberry I wanted. I expect she felt like spoiling me. I looked at my face in my compact mirror. I used to have really rosy cheeks from all the fresh air, now I couldn't go out without blusher. Still, I supposed I was pale and interesting. Otherwise, there wasn't much difference on the outside. *Inside* was the trouble.

I had to go through the shop again, as Ralph kept the back entrance locked. Now I knew why. I thought of the woman who had stolen the cookery books as, with a wave to Ralph, I walked out into the rain, pulling up my collar.

It was then I saw a traffic warden standing back as the black sports car tried to pull out into the traffic. She had a satisfied look and I could tell she had just given the driver a ticket.

I glanced at him as I passed. I could tell he was angry just by the way he sat. I couldn't see his face because of the lowness of the car and the spattering rain, but he had fair hair like Martin. . .

Trying not to think of the past, I attempted to cross the road. The traffic was heavy and the shoppers careless. I should have walked on up to the pedestrian crossing but it seemed too far.

I was going to take a chance, when I saw a man doing the same. An irate motorist honked at him. I decided I'd have to make for the crossing. I was heading towards *Mancini's Ristorante* over the road when the bleeps suddenly finished. I was angry with myself for being slow. I imagined everyone was looking at me. I tried to remember what the consultant had said.

"Keep on exercising the leg and you'll be fine. You'll get used do it. You will. Don't give up."

"I really have tried. I really have," I told myself as I looked into Mancini's.

There wasn't an empty table.

I just didn't want to go in there anyway. It held too many memories. I wanted to be by myself - away from everyone.

* * *

CHAPTER 3

The rain had stopped. It was cold for a summer's day as I turned away from Mancini's, towards St Martin-in-the-Fields. Perhaps there'd be a lunchtime concert. I could just sit and listen.

When I reached the steps, I knew I was unlucky so, negotiating the traffic once more, I walked into Trafalgar Square. There were lots of empty, wet benches. I sat down, having brushed away the rain with a handkerchief.

More people were pouring into Trafalgar Square now the rain had eased. The square was coming alive once more. The cascading fountains drew the damp from the air while those black lions gazed aloofly into the distance as of sensing old battles.

I could remember the dates by heart. Useless now. Down Whitehall, the lucky ones, in red capes, were keeping their restive black horses easy. I was thinking of the Cenotaph, and Martin again. How good an officer he'd have been if he hadn't been depressed. I thought of the agony he'd put his parents through, and that made me angry too. If only he'd asked for help. But he was too proud. And he'd nearly killed me. And ruined my life. I'd chosen a dangerous career but I'd never thought it would have ended this way. I shivered a bit thinking I ought to find some lunch and stop moping.

I wandered across the Square. On the corner was a hamburger stall. I bought a double bun just to cheer myself up from being so miserable. The rain was still holding off so I sauntered on, swinging my handbag as if I was happy, still trying to hide that tiny limp.

It was then I heard the drums. Their music always had a strange effect on me and, although tradition hadn't meant a lot to Martin, the sound of the drums brought that lump in my throat again. It was a quick march. I had kept up with it too many times to make a mistake.

They must be coming this way, but I couldn't see them yet. But they were soon there, swinging through the summer gloom, their red coats bringing the London scene to life. Other people had heard them now and were rushing towards the sound.

The scarlet coats of the Guards were nearer now. They were probably practising for Trooping the Colour, and I knew what it took to get that clockwork, soldier precision. I was aware of my leg that would not be doing any more marching.

A thrill seemed to run through the gathering crowd as the drum rolls increased. I was swallowing hard as they were almost on us, then, before I knew it, I could feel tears running down my cheeks. No-one heard me sniffing. No-one saw me wipe my eyes on my sleeve.

Suddenly, I was aware of someone standing very close. I could hardly see a thing through my tears except a blur of red tunics. The sound of the band thumped in my head as they swung away.

"Try this," a man's voice said. "Please?"

My English reserve told me to be careful, but I took the handkerchief and hid my burning face in its cool whiteness.

"I don't usually do this, you know," I muttered, my voice thick and muffled. I couldn't trust myself to look at him, very conscious that my nose would probably be red and my eyes puffy.

"I do," he replied.

It was such an unusual answer I had to look. The man was leaning against the wall directly behind me. I was too upset to take him in all at once, but my first impression was of a well-tanned, handsome face, topped by close-cut, fair hair. I saw he was built and dressed like an athlete, wearing track suit bottoms and a T-shirt, covered in damp patches.

"You mean you cry?" I asked.

He smiled. "Not usually in public. I know it's nothing to do with me, but what's the matter?" His expression became serious, as if he really wanted to know.

I came to my senses then. What was I doing here talking to a stranger? Not only was it foolish, it could be dangerous. I was ready to walk away.

"I don't want to talk about it," I said, looking at his handkerchief. It crossed my mind that I could be cracking up altogether.

"Well, why should you?" he remarked. "Put it down to the weather."

40

"Thank you. Here . . . you can have your handkerchief back. I'm all right now . . . Or should I keep it?" I smiled though I didn't feel like it.

"As a souvenir, you mean?" he asked. He was still leaning on the wall above me. I wondered whether he was out of breath from running. There was a strange look on his face, but he seemed disinclined to stretch out and take it from me.

"A souvenir of what? Of breaking down in the street?" I could not help the resentful remark.

"Please, keep it. You might need it again."

I thrust the handkerchief in my pocket sheepishly. His remark evidently showed he'd sensed my bitterness. I felt angry and foolish.

"Thanks," I said. "Bye then."

"Hold on a minute. One good turn deserves another."

I was on my guard immediately. He was biting his lip, as if he was in pain.

"Will you hand me my stick? There." He pointed. "I dropped it when the band went by." I saw the stick lying on the ground. I don't know why I hadn't noticed it before. I supposed because it was the grey colour of the stone. It was just an ordinary orthopaedic one with holes in. "I find it a bit difficult bending down."

"That's OK," I replied, trying to sound normal and not surprised.

It hurt my leg as I bent to pick it up for him, and suddenly, I wanted to laugh. Ironic. I'd been trying to learn to bend my knees like a lady, but it was hard with my disability. A sharp, little pain stabbed me as

I retrieved his stick, but I got it first time. "There you are."

The young man took it. I could tell by the look on his face that he had hated asking me to pick it up, but was grateful to have it again. He placed it carefully in front of him just like I used to, so he could get his balance. Instinctively, I reached out to help.

"No, I'll do it myself." His voice wasn't friendly any more.

I stood back, knowing just how he felt. I seemed like an interloper watching an act that ought to have taken place in private.

"I'm quite all right," he said.

But I just knew he was going to slip. He wasn't accustomed to using it, I could tell. I couldn't do a thing because he wouldn't let me. He fell heavily across the pavement and I heard him swear under his breath. There was a crack in his voice too. He was near to tears. I recognised the signs. People were going past, staring, then looking away, leaving the two of us alone.

"Look," I said decidedly, "I'm going to help you, whatever you say. You're behaving like an idiot. You know you need a leg up."

"A leg up!" His tone was scornful, but I gripped his arm and held it until he scrambled to his feet. Then he had to regain his balance. At one point, I thought I'd fall down as well because I didn't think I had the strength to manage, being so unfit.

"Right. We're quits."

He held out his hand to me and I could see he'd grazed the palm. I took it. It was a strong hand, warm and firm.

"Thank you."

I wanted to laugh again but that would have been as bad as crying. Here I was offering help and comfort to someone just as badly off as I was, but he didn't know that. Yet he must have caught the half-smile on my lips. He smiled back, using the stick to take him slowly along the pavement, back in the direction of the Square.

"Do you like the gear?" he asked, pointing to the track suit.

I did laugh then. It reminded me of myself when I used to take out an athletic strip after the accident and do some pretending.

"Yes, I do. Did you have a good run?"

He wasn't offended because suddenly, we were both laughing. I surprised myself then. It had been ages since I'd had a real joke - and enjoyed it.

"Richard Main," he said, holding out his hand again.

"Alison Dean," I replied.

We shook hands. It started to drizzle. We both looked at the grey sky.

"Summer," I grimaced.

In the distance, I could still hear the faint sound of drums. They were probably on the parade ground now. He heard them too.

"Magnificent, weren't they? What a spectacle. And can't they keep time?"

"They've had plenty of practice," I said.

"I suppose they have. Are you interested in the military then?"

"Only as an observer. I had just popped out for lunch."

"In the rain?"

"Oh, I don't have far to go," I said, the old wariness suddenly coming back.

"You're about to be caught in it again." The rain was coming on fast now and neither of us could run. "I should run if I were you," he added.

"It's OK, I'm only going up there. Shaftesbury Avenue."

"And I ought to get moving as well."

"Have you far to go?"

When I said that, I knew I was trying to prolong the conversation. After all, this stranger was the one I'd been closest to for a very long time.

"The car's parked just up there." He pointed, and I began to walk off. I expect he wondered why I didn't hurry, but I couldn't. The pain in my knees was almost unbearable.

"Goodbye," I called, turning.

He waved. Then, suddenly, I could hear him shouting, "How far did you say you were going, Alison?"

I slowed gladly, because I was so tired. He was hurrying to catch me up.

"Shaftesbury Avenue. I work in my cousin's bookshop."

I regretted it as soon as I'd said it. I was being stupid. He could be up to no good. But he didn't look like a threat. He had hair as blond as Martin's and if it hadn't been for the stick, I would have said he was a sportsman. He also had a wonderful smile.

"Well, as I told you the car's parked round the corner. I could drop you off. Which bookshop? I was up there earlier." He must have noticed my look. "Oh,

I'm sorry. That was stupid of me. I realise you wouldn't go in a car with a stranger."

We stood foolishly, with the rain plastering our hair and running off our faces.

"No, I wouldn't," I said. But I knew I would have given anything to be even more foolish at that moment. Richard Main had become a kind of lifeline. We walked on together round Trafalgar Square.

"Ah, there," he said, feeling in his pocket and drawing out his keys. I looked for the car, knowing he was still offering the lift. But I had no intention of going. It was then I heard the tiny bleep. I looked again, and panicked.

The black, shiny sports car was tucked very tightly into a space, its side lights responding to the driver's remote control; its shining eyes of lights slipping off their hooded eyelids in response to their master's orders.

I backed away. I could see the look on Richard Main's face as I turned and, limping, ran, like a crazed child, along the pavement, across the narrow road, on to the traffic island and towards the National Gallery.

I heard a car honking angrily at my carelessness, but I didn't care. I ran on, with the rain driving into my face, trying to put as much distance as I could between myself and that sinister Porsche.

And, all the time, I could see his amazed look as I ran away from him, a face that kept merging with the handsome face of Martin, who had killed himself and had crippled me in the same kind of car. I couldn't get away fast enough. . .

I slowed down finally, realising just how stupidly I'd behaved. Besides, my leg hurt so much I thought I'd done it some lasting damage, and all because of a man and a car that reminded me of Martin and the accident.

Whatever would Richard Main think about me, running off like that? I'd never been so rude before. I could hear my heart beating in my ears, and tried to calm myself. What did it matter anyway? I would never see him again. Strangely, that thought didn't cheer me up at all.

I stood miserably in the rain thinking that it wasn't likely that a disabled man would do me any harm. The thought brought me to with a jolt. Who was I to call him disabled? I was myself, only I didn't use a stick because I didn't choose to. I was lucky really.

"He probably thinks you're some hysterical female, Dean," I told myself sharply.

That was no consolation either. I looked down at the low, stone wall beside the flight of steps that led up to the National Gallery. It was wet and slippery.

Quite deliberately, I swept the rain aside with my hand and sat down disconsolately. All I could think of was that I been offered his handkerchief to dry my tears. I felt for it in my pocket. I brought out the crumpled square of fine cotton and looked at it. Suddenly, I was smiling. The monogram in the corner read, DMN.

Perhaps I'd been right and that mysterious stranger had criminal tendencies - hanky snatching. DMN certainly didn't stand for Richard Main. I suddenly found the bizarre meeting and the way I'd reacted extremely funny, and I began to giggle. It was probably a nervous reaction.

People were passing me on the steps all the time, giving me a wide berth. They probably thought I'd flipped, seated on a wall of the National Gallery, laughing, in the pouring rain. Yet no-one cared.

I could have sat all day crying or laughing. It was only once in a lifetime that anyone might ever notice or be caring enough to hand over a handkerchief. I scrubbed my face with it and put it back in my pocket.

Looking back briefly towards the Mall, I realised that Richard Main's kindness had been the first I'd responded to since the accident. I had laughed and it had been spontaneous.

It was then I wondered how many times he had felt just like me, standing against a wall, not daring to move, having to ask a passer-by to retrieve his stick. It hurt a lot. How much more had it hurt when I'd taken to my heels like an idiot.

It was then that I remembered where I should have been - back at work. A quick look at my watch confirmed how late I was and sent me walking as quickly as I could in the direction of the bookshop.

I felt really guilty. Ralph had been so kind, and I seemed to be taking advantage of his goodness in every way.

Each step I took then was in pain. I had done too much, of course. I would need painkillers when I got back. Then I realised I'd left them at home. I felt bedraggled and miserable once more.

All at once, I knew the depression was creeping again and there was certainly nothing more depressing than pushing through crowds of people in the pouring rain.

At that moment I saw *her*. I was so sure it was the woman who had run off with our books that I hurried to follow, and almost collided with her as she stopped suddenly to look in a shop window. She turned. The woman's face was quite blank and unrecognisable. I had been wrong and felt quite ridiculous. I hurried on.

Suddenly, I began to tell myself that I had to pull myself together. The damage had been done - losing the books; running away from a nice guy; the accident; Martin's death.

It was all history now and there was nothing on earth anyone else could do about it except myself. . .

* * *

CHAPTER 4

The shop was still full and Ralph was seated behind the counter. I hurried over to join him. "I'm sorry I'm late, Ralph."

I felt really guilty. He blinked at me from behind the thick lens of his glasses.

"Why? What time is it?"

My cousin hadn't even noticed. He wasn't angry, only concerned.

"You look all-in, Ally. You did have some lunch?"

"Of course," I lied.

"Pity I advised you to go out. You're soaked through," he said, staring at my raincoat.

He was so kind. I didn't deserve it.

"Only outside. This is a smashing mac."

"Looks very nice, dear. Oh, there's another thing."

"Yes?"

"You missed a visitor."

"A visitor? To see me?"

My heart gave a funny, little jerk. Could it have been Richard Main? I knew I wasn't being sensible. He didn't know which shop I worked in.

"She said she'd come back in the afternoon."

I was puzzled.

"She?"

"Yes. She said she was a friend of yours, from Sandhurst. She was on leave. She'd phoned your mother first, then ended up here."

"Who was it? What did she look like?"

I was trying to think who would come to see me now. Sandhurst seemed years ago.

"Hardly noticed. But wait a minute."

He was smiling faintly.

"Yes, now I come to think of it, she was quite nice-looking. Blonde, and good legs."

It was a full smile now. I grinned too. Ralph always said he was too busy to notice anything or anyone, especially women.

"Well, I reckon it's Tara. She fits the description"

Tara had been a fanatic about the Army as well. She'd also been very upset when she'd heard about Martin and me. But what was she doing in London? She was supposed to be abroad. I expected she would call back. Tara was reliable.

A few months ago, I wouldn't have wanted her to visit me. It was a bit like jealousy. I supposed that being glad to see her now was because I was resigned to the fact I'd never get back to Army life.

Suddenly, the events of the last hour were flooding back, like the rain and my tears . . . pictures of that moment when the Guards passed by me. The sympathetic face of Richard Main kept on rising in front of me as I began the monotonous work of wrapping purchases and answering queries. . .

We were so busy in the afternoon that I'd almost forgotten about my visitor until I looked out the window to see the rain had stopped, that a faint sunlight was filling the shop, that the customers were thinning and a blonde girl was coming through the door, a smile on her face.

Ralph was right. Nice-looking, blonde, excellent legs, poised and confident, more like a model than an officer in the British Army.

"Tara!"

"Alison!"

We hugged each other.

"What are you doing here?"

"It's my first real leave since posting. I had to come and find you. I've heaps to tell you."

I remembered so many things as I talked to Tara. We had met for the first time one cold, January morning. I remember being surprised to see such a fragile girl, because I thought one had to be pretty tough to get into the Army. She had looked as though the wind would blow her away.

I soon learned better. We had run in out of the wind together and stayed together. And I'd been quite mistaken. She was one of the fittest of the year, even fitter than some of the men. Under that porcelain exterior was a strength and an energy it was often difficult to keep up with. I was fit, but not like her. She could stand almost anything - the mud, the cold, the exercises. Yes, Sandhurst made a good choice with Tara. She played hard, too. The lads liked her a lot, but she hadn't found anyone special. But she had now.

51

I was mad to know who. He'd have to be good. We smiled at each other over our coffee cups.

"I think my Ralph's a saint. This is the second break I've had today. I'm really lucky."

I said that because I didn't want her pity. Here she was telling me about how much she was enjoying everything, and I only had memories. She was a real friend. I had met her family and she'd met mine. My parents were impressed, not only because she was a very nice girl but that her father was a brigadier. Tara had told me once that was were she'd inherited her tough streak. I believed her because he was awesome.

"Alison, eh? Army family?"

Whatever I'd answered had been approved and, after that, I'd been a regular and welcome visitor to their lovely home near Camberley.

Tara didn't have any brothers. She was an only child and I think that, like Martin, she, too, had felt she had the family tradition to follow.

I smiled at her that Saturday afternoon as we drank our coffee. How could I fail to be happy to see her after all the good times we'd shared?

"I'm glad to see you looking so well," she said.

I suppose I did. The last time Tara had seen me I was lying in hospital, all pinned, plastered and bandaged.

"Thanks. I feel it. You look great, too"

"I should," she replied.

She looked round and there was a sparkle in her eyes as if everything she was seeing was new. I recognised the look. Tara was in love. She stared straight at me then.

"You do look well," she added, "but, being so near to you now, I'm not sure if it's true. I don't mean physically but. . ." Tara always said what she meant.

"Go on," I replied quietly. "What do you see?"

"It will get easier, Alison. They say time heals." Her words were coming out in a rush.

"It must get better, it must." I bit my lip as I spoke, then, suddenly, all those pent-up feelings came pouring out.

I told Tara about the events of my day - the Guards marching down the Mall, about how I'd stood crying, but I didn't mention Richard. I couldn't. That had been one of those private, precious moments, when two people, strangers, had met on common ground. I stared at the table, thinking how we'd parted because of my stupid inability to face the reality of my situation.

Tara's hand closed over mine in sympathy. I could feel her pity, and I didn't want it.

"Sorry, Tara. It just came over me."

She nodded. "It's all right. It'll do you good. That kind of thing has to come out. Makes you better."

I felt selfish at that moment. Here she was, ready to tell me good news, and I was thinking only about my own feelings.

"Please, forget it," I said. "What's new in your life then?"

I could see the relief in her eyes. She let go of my hand and drank some more coffee.

"Well, Germany's great. Lots of teething troubles over the command, but nothing serious. It felt really strange in the beginning, taking charge of all those soldiers. There's only one other woman officer on base."

I laughed, imagining the impact Tara must have had on the men.

"The social life's absolutely fantastic, and I love the work. Are you sure you want me to go on, Alison?"

"Yes," I replied firmly. "I want to hear all about it - and about him."

She told me everything, including the details of the someone special in her life, who was in London on leave as well, and that he'd asked her to marry him.

He was Army, as I knew he would be, and was older and fairly high-up - a major at thirty-two.

"You don't think he's too old?"

I smiled at her question. All of Tara's training evidently hadn't prepared her for love. And she was certainly in love with Peter. I could see that. Suddenly, I wondered if I would ever feel like that, be really in love. I knew now that what I'd felt for Martin hadn't been that. I'd been mistaken all along.

"Of course he's not too old," I replied. "I assume you accepted?"

"When he asked me to marry him?" Tara hesitated.

"What did you say, Tara?"

"I said yes, but added I was going on with my career. It was a bit of a shock to him. At first, I was afraid he wasn't going to agree and then I'd have known it was no good between us. But he said he wouldn't stand in my way and he always knew I wanted to be a success. But I know it'll be difficult."

"Good for you, Tara. And congratulations. I'm happy for you, very happy. When's the wedding?"

"Hold on. We're only at grass-roots level yet. We're only about to get engaged. I wish things could have worked out for you, too, Alison. I really do." There was a slight awkwardness then she added, "And that's why I'm here. We're having an engagement party, tomorrow evening, in the mess at Salisbury. Peter's down there at the moment. We want you to come. Peter knows all about you."

That was what I was afraid of. They all knew about me, pitied me. But Tara looked so happy.

"Well, I don't know. It's a bit difficult at such short notice."

My excuses were as lame as I was. Tara looked very disappointed. I swallowed. It wasn't Tara's fault she was happy, and how much longer was I going to keep running away? I'd asked myself that once already today. She was hoping. I could see it in her face.

"We really want you to come. It'll be all right. There'll be one or two other people from Civvy Street."

She meant other civilians like me, and I had to get it out of my head I was still an Army officer. I got angry with myself then. I would go. I looked her straight in the eyes. "Right, I'll come. Thank you for asking me, Tara."

"You will?" She seemed delighted. "I know it's short notice. Do you want someone to pick you up?"

"Of course not. I can still drive."

I was determined I would get back behind the wheel. The car had been gathering dust, like me. A jaunt down the motorway would do us both good.

"What time?" I asked brightly, draining my cup.

"Seven-thirty for eight. Oh, is there anyone you'd like to bring?"

"No-one. I'll come on my own."

"I know you'll like Peter, Alison."

"I know I will," I replied.

Suddenly I thought about Richard Main. . .

"What did your friend with the lovely legs want?" Ralph asked. "Did you enjoy yourself?"

I nodded and smiled, patted his arm and followed him as he went outside to the front of the shop. He wasn't the least put-out that I'd wasted half the working day and lost him some expensive books. How was I going to ask him for Monday off now? I'd never be able to go to the party on Sunday night and get back from Wiltshire and straight into work. Not in my state of health. I frowned and I could see Ralph watching me.

I knew I'd been a misery as well. As I helped bring in the books which had been standing on long shelves under the awning, I promised myself that next week would be different.

"Tara invited me to her engagement party."

It was Ralph's turn to smile. His eyes twinkled.

"No chance for me then," he joked. "Are you going?"

"I'd like to, but it's tomorrow evening in Salisbury."

"Well, what's stopping you? It's not the end of the world."

I swallowed. "But I'll never make it for opening on Monday."

"Well, come in on Tuesday then," he replied. He was a very nice man indeed.

"Are you sure, Ralph? I'm a hopeless assistant, aren't I?"

"No, but you can be horribly negative sometimes. I want you to go. Now will you?" He looked just like my mother when he said it. I nodded, he continued. "Good, and about time. Now let's get on with this."

I followed him back inside. When we'd cleared the front, it was getting near closing. Customers were pretty thin and we walked through to the kitchen. While Ralph sat by the door, so he could see if anyone came in, I boiled the kettle. He looked at me carefully.

"Now," he said, "you can tell me to mind my own business if you want. Remember, I'm not your mother, thank goodness. First of all, you don't have to keep apologising to me. I realise this isn't your idea of an exciting life. It wasn't mine once."

I was surprised. I thought Ralph was happy doing what he'd been doing for years.

"And I don't mean bookselling," he added. "I had to get over it, too, you know, when my wife died. I needed to do this, something to take my mind off her death. We all have to concentrate on something."

I felt ashamed of how self-centred I had been with him.

"I know what you're thinking about all the time, little cousin," he went on. "The Army and Martin. I never met the bloke, but I can't help thinking he wanted to do what he did. That was up to him. But he shouldn't have tried to take you with him."

Suddenly, I could feel my hands shaking. I didn't know whether from fear or anger.

"Now, the Army. That is different. I know all about life in the Services."

It was true. Ralph had been in the Army once.

"I don't blame you grieving for it, but you seem to think you're on the shelf now, like all those books."

He gestured towards the shop, and I managed a watery smile. "But you're not, girl. You're not."

He put an arm round my shoulders and suddenly drew me to him. There was no embarrassment between us. I just laid my head on his shoulder, glad of the comfort, glad to listen to the good sense he was handing out.

"I've wanted to say this ever since you came here. The Army was going to be your life, but it isn't the only life, Alison. There are lots of other people out there, lots who don't have anything at all. Some have lost everything. There are even those who can't walk at all. If you do what the doctors told you to do, you'll be as good as new - not even a limp. But it takes time. Believe me."

I felt ashamed. Ralph seemed to be almost talking to himself. I lifted my head and nodded. He had tears in his eyes. I put up a hand and touched his cheek. He took my hand and held it there. Then we hugged each other.

"I'm trying, Ralph. And I'm going to win. I am."

It was then we both heard the shop bell tinkle. Ralph let me go gently.

"Sorry, love. Someone's come in."

He was looking at his watch. It was always the same. Someone always came in just at closing, and they were nearly all time-wasters.

"OK. Shall I make a cuppa?" I asked.

He nodded.

"Three sugars?"

"Of course."

"I'll bring it out to you," I called.

When I walked back through with the cuppa there was no sign of Ralph. Putting down the mug, I walked round the book stacks, looking for him. I stared, blinking and stared again as Ralph put the large book on the Napoleonic Wars back on the Military Section shelf and smiled at me.

"Tea up then, Alison?"

His customer was smiling, too. He was fair-haired and leaning heavily on his stick. The track-suit trousers had been replaced by fashionable cords, but the smile was the same.

I gasped as Richard Main's eyes held mine.

"You two know each other then?" Ralph said and there was a roguish note in his voice I had never heard before.

* * *

CHAPTER 5

"We have met."

I was glad Richard Main had answered. I wouldn't have known what to say even if I could have found the words. All I kept asking myself was how did he know where I worked? He must have followed me.

"Recently?" Ralph asked.

"Actually," Richard replied, "today. I met Alison in the Mall."

I could see the wary look in Ralph's eyes.

"That's nice. In the Mall?" he repeated, looking at Richard carefully.

I couldn't just stand there staring. I offered Ralph his mug.

"Thanks, Alison." He was still staring at Richard fixedly, almost as if he knew him from somewhere..

"We met by accident," Richard was saying as I looked at his stick. "Alison was kind enough to give me a hand. I was watching the parade and my stick was inaccessible. We made each other's acquaintance afterwards."

It all sounded so ordinary, but there had been nothing ordinary about our meeting.

"I see," Ralph said. "Two military historians together."

I could see the startled look on Richard Main's face.

"So you told Mr Main that I had some very interesting books back here. Thanks, Alison. I always enjoy meeting knowledgeable customers. Very nice to find a specialist on the war in Korea. He's got his eye on these. Knows a bargain."

Ralph was an old fox. His eyes were glinting again behind his spectacles as he handed the books to Richard. He was determined to find out about this young man. He had more sense than I did. My brain was working on a purely emotional level. I had to either agree or deny I'd told Richard about the shop. I side-tracked.

"Yes, these are a real bargain, although the Korean War's not really my field," I replied, and Ralph must have caught the edge in my voice because he picked up his cup and spoke with a meaningful look.

"Well I'm sure Alison will be able to give you any further help you need. I'll be round there if you want me."

He walked off, his eyes twinkling. What would he have said if he'd known the two of us were strangers? I almost called Ralph back because I felt panicky. Maybe making casual acquaintance like this had been risky. But perhaps Richard hadn't tried to find me. Perhaps it was just coincidence, him coming into the shop. I pulled myself together, looking at the book he was holding.

"How did you know where I worked?" I regretted the question immediately. He now had a quizzical look.

"I didn't. I just took a chance."

The statement seemed quite unlikely. I should have been on my guard but, all the time I was talking to him, my heart was giving funny, little jumps. There was an undeniable, irresistible attraction in the way we were reacting towards each other.

"Don't you believe me?" he added.

I swallowed then took the book from him as he held it out. Our fingers brushed in contact sending further shocks through me.

"But there are dozens of bookshops round here," I replied, re-shelving the book and looking at the other titles while trying to hide my confusion.

"Let's say I did a little detective work then."

I turned to see he was shifting from one foot to the other. I wanted to ask him to sit down, but I couldn't. He was probably in pain, but he was still smiling.

"Detective work?" I could have held his smile in my eyes for ever. He was really a gorgeous-looking guy. And he'd come looking for me. "What do you mean?" I added, hoping my voice sounded normal.

"I mean that, as I'm an expert on the Korean War and that this is the best second-hand bookshop in the area dealing with the conflict, I decided to try here first. I actually parked here earlier on. I work in this area. it was pouring with rain and I found a space right outside. I could see the display. I promised myself I'd come back."

I was full of relief as I remembered the black sports car I'd spotted outside this morning, the car that had made me remember Martin. That I should meet the driver was far too eerie for coincidence.

His eyes were fixed on my face, as if trying to remember something.

"There was another reason though."

"Oh?" My voice sounded so little-girlish but he was having a very strange effect on my emotions.

"I just felt, when I met you, that someone who was so stirred-up by those soldiers marching might have some special feeling for the Army. Or links with it? Or something?"

I was amazed. Was the man a psychologist, or a psychic? No, he'd probably followed me. Quite simple. My face burned, thinking of the crazy way I'd run from him and his car.

"I'm right, aren't I?" he went on. "I can tell it meant something to you, the way you were crying," he added softly.

"I don't know what to think," I said.

How could all this be happening? It was like a romantic novel. Women were supposed to be the intuitive ones. Perhaps this Richard Main was just a very good actor.

"But am I right?" he was persisting.

I always feel angry when I'm about to panic, and the feeling was mounting.

"I'm afraid I can't tell you that. . ." I hesitated. "I prefer to think it was luck."

"OK, I'll go along with that. Do you remember earlier on when you were crossing the road?"

"That's it. You saw me," I accused.

"Yes. I couldn't miss you. That blasted traffic warden wouldn't take any notice of what I said. I was really steamed-up. But I was lucky I wasn't clamped.

63

"And there was this crazy girl coming out of the shop, dodging through the traffic dangerously. You ought to be more careful in the rain. And, then, as Fate would have it, there I was standing, watching the Guards and whom should I see again? So, when you said you worked in a bookshop up Shaftesbury Avenue, I put two and two together."

"I get it," I replied, my stomach fluttering.

I supposed I should have been feeling flattered, but the only emotion flooding through me was sheer excitement that he'd come to look for me. I tried to hide my feelings. Crazy moments didn't happen to me any more. They were dangerous. this was madness. He was touching my arm.

"I'm glad, Alison, I really am. I couldn't pass up the chance. I wanted to see you again. Why did you run away from me like that? Did you think I was dangerous? Hardly." He was looking at his stick. "I suppose I could have felled you with one blow."

The corners of his lips were curved in that wonderful smile, a smile a girl could fall in love with.

"You look as though you might be pleased as well."

I turned in confusion. I couldn't just stand there while this stranger paid me compliments which made my nerves tingle and gave me such thrilling feelings inside.

"Please, say something." His hand was on my arm.

"It's almost closing time. Do you want any of these books or not?"

We both started to laugh, and Ralph appeared from round the corner.

"What's the joke?"

I could see the pleasure on his face. He hadn't seen me like this for ages.

"Oh, I see. Private."

Richard Main had two books in his hand. "I'll take these, please. I've been looking for the first for some time. When did you get it?"

"Oh, someone came in a couple of weeks ago and I snapped it up. It's the definitive work," Ralph answered.

"Well, I've no idea when I'll get time to read it, I'm very busy."

They chatted on as I walked in front of them towards the till. Had he noticed I limped when I ran away earlier, or could he see my limp now, I wondered. While Ralph wrapped the books, I stood at the till feeling slightly foolish. It was then Richard must have seen his advantage.

"Closing up now?" He placed his stick against the counter.

Ralph nodded. "Yes. It's always like this after the rain. People just want to get off home. Can't blame them." He handed over the books. "That's fifteen pounds, please."

"A bargain," Richard replied, opening an expensive, leather wallet and pulling out the cash.

While he was doing so, he was trying to hold his stick against the counter with his other knee. I knew how every simple thing became difficult when one was disabled.

His stick fell again. He was obviously quite a novice at using it. We both moved to retrieve it at the same time, and he was looking me straight in the eyes as we both straightened.

"I wonder - do you have to hurry home, Alison? Perhaps you'd like to have dinner with me?"

How could I refuse. I wanted to more than anything. "Well, I do have to go home. But I suppose I could come back."

"You go out, Alison," Ralph interrupted. "It'll do you good. I'm sure Mr Main intends to look after you."

Richard withdrew a card from his wallet and handed it to Ralph.

"My address and telephone number just in case you get any more of the series in. I'd be grateful."

He turned to me. I was glad he'd given Ralph the card. Now someone else knew who he was.

"So what shall we say? I can come and pick you up if you like, from home."

"No, that'll be all right. Ralph's running me home now and I'll come back in on the train later. It's quite useful really. My parents are taking in a show this evening and we'll travel up together."

It was my military training. I was taking no chances. As we made the arrangements to meet, I was squashing that tiny fear inside, which kept trying to rise and choke me - the fear of ever taking the plunge again; of perhaps starting a relationship, where, sooner or later, I was going to have to reveal how I truly felt.

* * *

We met at a small, intimate Italian restaurant just off Piccadilly Circus. Pepino's had an excellent reputation and the food was marvellous.

I felt a thrill when I walked in with Richard by my side, and it didn't matter that he was so awkward with his stick. He seemed to have got over worrying about it too. I still didn't know what he'd done, and whatever it was, he covered it well. He appeared to be very fit, looking sophisticated in very trendy clothes. The way he walked impressed me as well. It must have taken a lot of willpower to hold himself so straight when he was probably in some pain.

Suddenly, I was thinking of the way the Guards had swung down the Mall. Could Richard have been a soldier some time?

We laughed a lot during the meal and I found myself relaxing in a way I thought could never again happen with a man.

"This is lovely," I said, and I was referring to the meal. It was the first time I had felt so happy in ages, and there was something else, too.

I had told Richard all about the accident and Martin, which was certainly surprising. I never mentioned my affair with him if I could help it. It was too painful. I had also broken a promise to myself, that I wouldn't pour out my past. But it was so easy to talk to this fair-headed, young man who leaned towards me sympathetically, making me feel as if I was the most important person in the whole world. He was very, very charming.

"I'm glad you're enjoying it here," he replied. "I am. I usually come to Pepino's. It has atmosphere. Besides, the food's excellent."

I smiled. A small twinge of fear had speared me as we had begun the main course, not because of anything he said but, strangely enough, in the way he ate. It was almost as if he was indeed a soldier.

At Sandhurst, we were trained to eat meals fast, on the double, as if every one was our last. I didn't remark on the fact. It would have been too rude, but I was curious to find out more about Richard, the military historian. However, I had been too busy offloading my troubles. I felt ashamed and a little worried that I'd been either a bore or indiscreet.

"I'm sure I've talked too much," I said, taking the menu the waiter was offering. "Oh, gosh, I don't know whether I can manage a sweet."

Richard was laughing.

"Don't worry, please. I've enjoyed our conversation so much. And go on . . . have something more. You won't put on weight. If you don't mind me saying so, you have a great figure."

As he filled my wine glass again, I was trying to take hold of myself. Why was I finding this man so attractive? I had decided I would stay on my own for a very long time and, now, here I was falling into the old trap once more.

"I really have, you know," he said, placing the wine bottle back in its cooler.

"Pardon?"

"Enjoyed listening to you. I'm glad you told me about the Army, Alison. It all makes sense now. You shouldn't be ashamed of crying about things you care for. I told you that I cry sometimes, didn't I? Remember, it doesn't do any good to bottle up the emotions. They're best out. And, if it's any consolation, I had no idea there was anything the matter with your legs. They look great as well."

"But what about you?" I asked.

"That's a very uninteresting subject," Richard replied.

"Please, that's not fair," I said. "I've told you all about myself. It's your turn."

"Not much to tell. I come from a military family, hence the interest. My grandfather was in the Korean War. Glorious Gloucesters. He didn't come back."

Richard's tone was quiet, and I was angry with myself for prying. "I'm sorry," I said hurriedly to cover my awkwardness.

"Don't be. My father grew up wanting to be a soldier, but not getting his way. Mother couldn't bear the idea. I think he was hoping I'd follow in Grandad's footsteps. I didn't. Only read it all up in books. I made it a hobby, but the rest of the family are committed."

"What do you do, Richard?" I asked.

Strangely, it hadn't occurred to me to ask before.

"Arts and media."

"Oh?" I was really surprised.

"Can be exciting, too. A little too hairy sometimes. I can vouch for that." He was staring down at the table, then looked up to face me. "But, at the moment, I'm not doing much."

"You mean . . ." I was looking at the stick.

"Yes. Let's say that, after the last sortie, I'm preparing myself for the next."

I realised he wasn't going to tell me what had happened to him. It was written all over his face. Perhaps he'd injured himself on an assignment? I couldn't imagine. Could he be a stunt man, I wondered, or a journalist? Whatever he was, it was clear he couldn't work at the moment.

He was searching my face for reaction. He leaned over and took my hand. I let him hold it.

"All I can say is I'm lucky, Alison, luckier than a lot of others. Luckier than my grandfather, luckier than you. At least this is only going to be temporary."

When we had finished our sweets, I said, "I hope, you know, that I'm getting over my disability. Of course, I can't have the Army back, but that can't be helped. I have to get on with my life. In fact, I've decided to do something quite wild for what's left of this week-end."

He looked surprised.

"Yes, I agreed to go to a party, in the West of England, tomorrow. It's an old friend's engagement."

I was psyching myself up to ask him to come, too. But he never gave me the chance.

"Why, that's wonderful," he said. "Go and enjoy yourself. You deserve it. I hope you have a marvellous time. Will you be away long? I hope not, because I'd like to see you some time next week, if you can manage it. Coffee?"

I shook my head. The moment had passed.

There was no chance of asking him now. I could tell when someone was being casual. I'd had plenty of practice with Martin, and I was remembering how all the chasing had been done by me. Never again. I felt quite disappointed, even empty. I screwed up my napkin and placed it beside my plate.

"Thank you. That was marvellous. I can't remember when I last enjoyed an evening so much."

"Neither can I. Waiter? The bill, please."

Soon, I was collecting my things. It had been a wonderful evening but I had ended up spoiling it a little, at least, in my eyes. Once again, I was going too fast. "Jumping the gun," my old sergeant major would have said.

Richard insisted on taking me to Waterloo Station in a cab. I had told him I was going on home ahead of my parents. The subterfuge seemed so silly now. Why couldn't I have trusted him?

* * *

We stood on the platform, looking at the indicator board. He leaned on his stick and I was worried about how much his leg hurt. But Richard wouldn't leave until my destination went up. He was a perfect gentleman and I liked that, even though I was a tough, ex-Army officer and could look after myself.

When the board showed my train was in, I was about to put out my hand to shake his. He looked down and smiled. "Bit formal, isn't it?"

My heart gave a tiny leap. Next moment, his free arm had slipped round me. It was a moment like I'd never experienced. Anyway, that's what it felt like. His lips were warm and firm. I just closed my eyes and savoured the kiss. I used to be careful never to display my emotions in public but just then I couldn't have cared if the whole world had been watching us. I was sure he'd hear my heart thudding when we were close.

I couldn't imagine just how much a kiss would stir me or how much I wanted it. I knew I was going to have to run for the train, but I would have given anything to stay. After that seemingly-endless moment, he let me go, looking as shaken as I felt.

There was something in Richard's eyes I'd never seen before. Tenderness? Desire? I'd never seen a look like that in Martin's. My heart was racing even faster. Pure attraction? I knew I wanted him and he wanted me.

"I must see you again," he whispered, our faces very close.

"Yes, I feel the same way," I answered, my head whirling. We started to walk to the barrier.

"Shall I come to the shop?"

"Yes, please." It was then I realised I hadn't given him my phone number or address.

"Just come in next week. And thank you, for everything."

Suddenly, there were so many tears pricking my eyes, I could hardly see. I swallowed, glanced up at the indicator screen through a haze of tears, hoping he hadn't noticed. He squeezed my arm.

"Goodbye, Alison. Thank you. It's been a wonderful evening." I felt his light kiss on my cheek this time.

I glanced back at Richard as I went through the barrier. He was still watching me leaning on his stick. He put up one hand and waved.

At that moment, I could have really let go the tears, but why? Were they tears of happiness, or regret for everything I'd lost? Feeling choked with emotion and wishing I had Richard's handkerchief once more, I turned and hurried as quickly as I could towards the waiting train.

CHAPTER 6

Sunday morning found me packing for my expedition. I would have liked to have worn a short skirt for Tara's party but, although I had legs for it, I was still conscious of remaining scar marks.

Instead, I packed a full, long-line skirt in black. However, I had decided to compensate for not revealing my legs by showing off my new slender waist line, and had bought a broad, evening belt to add a touch of glamour. A rather special silk top was slipped into my week-end bag to complete my outfit.

I'd kept my promise to myself to go by car, have lunch on the way and drive on to the Army camp at Salisbury from there, changing when I got there. I'd made a reservation at a nearby hotel for Sunday night. I'd stayed there once before and liked it a lot. There were wonderful open views of the Plain and, as I remembered, a dear little stream trickling through the grounds. I had many reasons for not wanting to stay on the camp with Tara. It would bring back too many memories. In fact, I had everything worked out properly.

"Alison, are you decent?" Mum peered round my bedroom door as I was putting the last few things into my case.

I nodded. She had tried everything earlier on to quiz me about my date with Richard. In fact, both of them had. At first, it had all been talk about the theatre but then the questions had come tumbling out. I didn't resent it because I knew they loved me and wanted me to be happy. It must have been hard for them after the accident.

"Was he nice?" Mum had asked eagerly.

"Very," had been my unhelpful reply.

"What's he do then?" That was Dad.

"Arts and media," I replied, waiting for the outburst.

"What the hell is that?"

Mum was looking at Dad. "Now, come on, Dad, we all can't be Commandos." I wish she hadn't said it though. "I'm sure this Richard has a very good job."

"Yes, he has," I replied, "but we didn't talk a lot about him. More about me."

"Lovely," Mum said, glancing in Dad's direction.

They were so funny. I could read their faces. They thought it was a good sign I'd opened up to someone. Thankfully, they left it there because they realised I was only going to tell them the minimum. I loved them too for trying to be diplomatic. Anyway, it was better that way as, with hindsight, I was beginning to feel sure nothing would come of Richard and myself. We were two different people. My world wasn't his.

"Is something the matter, dear?"

"No." I came back to the present with a jolt. "Just trying to decide if I have everything"

"Well, it's only for a night," said Mum. "I'm sure Tara will lend you anything you've forgotten. She's

74

such a nice girl. Imagine. She's getting married. I can hardly believe it."

"Why?" I said. That was one thing I didn't want - Mum reminiscing over the fun Tara and I had had in the past. I looked round. "I think that's everything. Come on, Mum."

Dad came to the bottom of the stairs as I limped down with my holdall. He tried to take it off me, but I shook my head. "No, I'm all right."

"And so's the car, Ally." He looked a bit hurt. "I've checked the oil and went round the garage and filled her up for you. Everything seems to be fine."

"Thanks." I said, immediately sorry I'd been so brusque. "I ought to go away more often." I always joked like that to hide my feelings

"Why don't you let me drive you down?" he added.

I shook my head.

"I could find something to do until very late," he persisted.

"No, Dad. Thanks for the offer, but I'm taking myself. Anyway, I've booked a bed for the night. Don't worry, either of you. I'll be okay. I'm quite looking forward to my little adventure." It was hard to keep the sarcasm from showing. Once I'd hoped to travel the world. Now my parents were worried in case I couldn't get as far as Salisbury. I felt sick and tired of myself and my illness.

"But you'll phone and let us know you've arrived, and if your driving leg gives you any trouble, Daddy will come down." Mum's look was full of anxiety.

"I will, of course." I picked up my holdall again and this time Dad didn't offer to help. Then Mum went into the kitchen and returned with a plastic bag.

"Here you are," she said.

"What is it?"

"In case you get thirsty on the way." I peeped inside. There was a flask and what looked like a packed lunch.

"Oh, thanks, Mum," I said and kissed her. "But there was really no need. I could have stopped somewhere."

"It's a long drive," said Dad.

They were really good and I was a misery not to appreciate them. One day, I'd tell them how much they meant to me.

Dad had left the car outside on the road and the two of them came with me to it. Mum kissed me goodbye, then Dad. It was ridiculous really - as if I was emigrating. They didn't say another thing, but only stood watching as I got into the car rather awkwardly.

They were still watching as I reversed down the drive and into the road and I knew they would watch until I was out of sight. I gritted my teeth inwardly at their protectiveness, but I was really glad that I had insisted on travelling by myself. However much I loved them, I had to get myself back on my feet.

* * *

When I finally found myself in Wiltshire, the sky was an ever-changing pattern of blowing clouds, which seemed to drift over the rolling, empty landscape. I'd forgotten just how desolate it could be on Salisbury Plain. I had come to a part where the wide strip of road met another on a T junction, looking like a straggly white cross scored into the fields. A bit past the junction, there was a lay by. Doubtless, the council had thought putting it there was a good idea as well as safe - so people could enjoy the view.

My leg was aching now and I decided to stop. I pulled off the road. I wanted to look at the countryside myself, to let its welcome isolation wash over me. How different it was from London. Here I could think, alone, unhindered. Whether that was a good thing or not, I didn't know.

As I dug deep into the carrier bag for the flask and my snack, I craned my neck to see where, above the car, a hawk was swooping over the ridge, plummeting down towards its unfortunate prey.

The wind rocked the car gently, its noise filling my ears with whining music. I poured the coffee and bit into my sandwich. It was then the memories flooded back. the time Tara had opened up. . .

I was remembering Martin so clearly that it brought tears to my eyes. Oh, why hadn't I listened to what Tara had told me about him? It had been a week or so before the accident. She must have sensed that one way or the other we were either going to call it a day or decide to get married. . .

"Ally," she said. I was sitting on the bed at the time, checking over my kit.

"Yes?"

"I know you'll think I'm poking my nose into your affairs but I have to say something to you. About Martin."

I froze. I was so sure now that I didn't want to hear. I was finding out for myself at last and I didn't want anyone else to cloud my judgement.

"Why do you? It's not your business."

"I know. But I have to say it. I don't think Martin's right for you." Her words came rushing out.

I just stared at her. She was biting her lip. Throughout our years of training, I'd never seen her look quite as upset. She came and sat on the bed beside me, swinging her legs and staring at her shiny black shoes.

"Go on, then," I said. "Spit it out." I stroked my belt buckle apprehensively.

"I've watched you these last months and - I care about you, Ally, I really do. Martin's not the man for you. I know it."

"Why?"

"I told you, didn't I, that I knew him years ago when we were kids."

"Yes. And that was years ago."

"And he hasn't changed. I know he hasn't. He's hard inside, Ally. He doesn't care about anyone or anything. Only himself. I could put up with his arrogance and his moods, but it's inside that counts. I think he's got a lot of hang-ups. He's off balance."

"Well, the Army didn't seem to think so and they're very good about sussing out psychological weakness," I said. I was making it particularly hard for her. One part of me wanted to know everything about him; the other, nothing.

"You still don't understand, do you?" pleaded Tara. "I mean what he's like with women. He doesn't like them, Ally. Not deep down. He despises them. And you wouldn't like that, would you? For ever."

I felt really cold then. "Despises women?"

"Yes." Tara was looking full at me now. Her eyes were bright with tears. "I know. Rather- I knew a girl. She was my friend at school. She was one of my brother's friend's sisters."

I drew in a breath.

"Her name was Izzy. Isobel. We used to call her Dizzy. She was great. A sweet kid. And she worshipped Martin. She was seventeen years old and she would have done anything for him. She'd had fantastic results in her GCSE's. She could do sports as well. One weekend - we were all invited to his house. It was his birthday. She was over the moon.

"On the Saturday night at his party, she'd been drinking. We'd all had a few, but not as much as Dizzy. And Martin was tanking her up. He knew how she felt about him . . ."

Tara had her hand on my arm now. I was waiting. Was Tara going to tell me they went to bed together or something? I was thinking of how they got past his mother. Perhaps the parents hadn't been there?

Tara breathed in deeply. I could see she intended to carry on. She added, "I tried to stop her - we all did - but Martin had her on a string. It was a really hot summer night and a lot of people were taking off their clothes. . . Quite a party really. Some of us were popping pills as well. But it was mostly alcohol."

"Where was his mother?"

"Oh, they were away for the weekend. They were always away. Anyway, Ally, things went from bad to worse. A lot of people made for the swimming pool. As you know, it's a big one. . ." It was. They had a diving board and everything. Tara continued, "Martin was in

79

his element. He was a championship swimmer, you know. Even then he was really showing off. And what did he do? Took poor Dizzy with him."

"What do you mean?" I shivered, thinking about our ride round Silverstone.

"Oh, she'd have done anything to impress him. And he dared her. She was a brilliant diver too. I can see her now. She'd taken off her bra and I tried to stop her climbing the ladder. But she wouldn't. And Martin was down below in the water, egging her on. The blokes were trying to stop him too."

"Was he drunk as well?" I managed to ask.

"Drunk with power." I knew what Tara meant. I could imagine his eyes shining. "And Dizzy leapt right off the top board. She was so drunk she didn't go straight in. She went crooked and hit her head on the second. It was terrible." We sat in silence, both imagining that awful moment. I didn't dare say anything. When Tara began speaking again, her voice was trembling slightly. "Misadventure. That was the verdict, Ally."

"You mean she died?"

"'Fraid so. But it should have been *murder*. Ally, Martin *killed* Dizzy. As much as if he smashed her head against that board himself. But who was to know? Only the people who were there. She'd been drinking. And people do stupid things when they're like that. *I* knew what Martin had done though. Poor Dizzy. Seventeen. What a waste."

Then Tara put her arm round my shaking shoulders and said firmly, "I had to tell you, Ally, before you do something stupid like marrying him. He hasn't changed, really he hasn't. I know. I can see it every day - and God help what battalion gets him. I just hope there isn't another war. Do you see what I mean now? *Do you*? I just couldn't stand by and let you marry him." She was looking me straight in the eyes. She was a very good friend. "Forgive me?"

"We're not thinking about getting married, Tara. Don't worry. I can handle myself." I couldn't forget the relieved look on my friend's face when I said that. . . And a week later Martin almost killed me. . .

. . . I shivered and, looking away from endless skyscape, I pulled myself into the present. Staring fixedly at the dashboard controls, I started the engine and turned up the heater. I didn't want to think of those long horrible days when I'd come out of the hospital. I'd been depressed too. Once, I'd sat in the garage at home with the doors closed and wondered if I shouldn't end it all.

At that moment, I knew I had to snap out of my self-pity. I was alive and I should be thankful. . . I shook my head and got myself together. I had to think of nice things.

As the temperature rose in the car and Mum's coffee warmed me, another face came up in my mind. Fair hair and handsome, with much kinder eyes than Martin. Suddenly, I became more optimistic. Why shouldn't we go out together? He had a bad leg too and he'd never complained about it. He managed really well.

"Yes, I'm going to think of you instead, Richard," I told myself out loud. "I'm going to be positive. I'll get through this party whatever I do." I switched to Radio

One and, pulling out of the lay-by on to the road, I accelerated up the thin string of a road on towards Salisbury, and lunch.

I did stop again, once, to look at the enormous regimental badges carved out of chalk on the side of a hill. One was of Mercury springing along on his winged feet and another of the Crown. How long did it take for some poor soldier to carve those? I smiled to myself at the thought. Anyway, they certainly let everybody know the Army was around.

I was still feeling optimistic when I discovered a small tea shop in the town centre, which had a lovely view of the cathedral's needle-point spire. Later, I went for a walk, glad to stretch my legs after the long drive. I stood on the bridge looking down at the river. As the water flowed along with my thoughts, I knew that a few miles from here I would be closer to my past again.

I wanted to make sure once more that I was ready, so I walked into the cathedral to calm myself. I sat in one of the pews and bowed my head. . .

I looked up and saw the tattered battle flags from days gone by. I knew I had a real fight on my hands and that what I was doing there in the stillness of the cathedral was asking for the confidence and the strength not to take fright and run back home again.

I found myself driving slowly through the woods now, where the sun was sending shafts of light through the leafy greenery, dappling the snake-like road. It was very quiet for an afternoon in summer, and I felt quite drowsy. Again my leg was aching. I was cross because I needed to stop again.

The next thing I caught sight of, made the last two years roll back very quickly - a road sign warning motorists of oncoming tanks.

There were great ruts in the wood on both sides of the road. The tank-crossing reminded me vividly of when I'd been whirled, thrilled and bumped along in one. It had been an experience I didn't care to repeat then, but now, I thought, if only I had the chance. But Tara and I had promised ourselves that we didn't want to end our days cooped up in a tank.

I sighed but, again, another thought was running fast through my mind - a thought that only a civilian could entertain. What a mess they made of those lovely woods.

About a mile farther up from the tank crossing, where the road was straight, I pulled into a large lay-by, protected by overhanging trees. On the other side of the road, the bank was high with hazel bushes; on my side the wood dropped away steeply.

I knew that, at the bottom, out of sight, was the camp's perimeter fence. I needed another breather before facing all my friends. Winding down my window just a bit, I sat, eyes closed, listening to the sounds of the birds. . .

I must have dropped off for about half an hour. Rubbing my eyes, I stretched, sat up and looked in the rear-view mirror. I could see another car parked behind me, about fifty yards away.

It was an especially eerie moment, almost as if time was standing still. My neighbour was a gleaming, black sports car. A Porsche. It had parked a little off the road, too, straddled in an untidy manner across some of the tracks the heavy artillery had made.

For one, cold second, as the driver's door opened, I thought I was about to see Martin stand and wave to me. Instead, the driver was stretching out and up. The sun glinted on the lens of the field glasses he was holding to his eyes. He was standing, tall and straight, the glasses fixed down into the woods, in the direction of the camp.

I gasped as he dropped the binoculars and came round to the passenger door which was opening. I wasn't interested in who was getting out. My mouth was dry. I stared, hardly believing my eyes, but there was no mistake. . .

It was Richard. Richard Main. Yet how could it be? Was I dreaming? Or mistaken? And, to my astonishment, he was walking easily round the car to the passenger, handing him the glasses, standing, chatting, laughing and hurrying. *There was no sign of a stick, no limp.* Then he was bending over the boot of the car while his companion, a fit looking, middle-aged man was helping to lift out some gear.

There was nothing wrong with Richard Main. He *was* fit. How could he be? What was going on?

Swallowing hard, I slumped down on my seat, my heart thumping, my mind racing. I felt sick, and cheated. What was he doing here? How could he be so close to me? This couldn't be coincidence? No. Then I remembered all the questions he'd asked me about the Army.

I began to feel faint. I would never have been as indiscreet when I was an officer. What had we said? I was racking my brains angrily. Had I told him that I was coming to Salisbury, to the camp? How could I have been such a fool?

In my mind I went over Saturday afternoon. How on earth *had* we met like that in the Mall? Could it have been planned? It seemed unthinkable. I had no access to the Army nowadays. But it was a horrible thought. And one never knew these days.

I was appalled at the implications. I should have been more careful, but it had all seemed so innocent. What I was thinking had to be a mistake. But what were they doing?

I watched as they put on heavy boots and walking gear. Then they slung packs on their backs and another light one which I knew was camera equipment. With one last look in the field glasses, the two men swung off downwards in a diagonal, disappearing into the sunlight trees.

I was very angry now and quite alert. How on earth could he pretend to be disabled on a Saturday and make a full recovery the very next day? Why had he been standing watching the Guards in London? Now here he was down in a sensitive area doing the same.

All the curt orders I'd taken and given about security in the past were filling my ears. Was there any way Richard could be in the Army, too, in spite of what he'd told me? No, it didn't make sense. . . Unless. . . It was too awful to contemplate. I had to alert the camp, but I wanted to know where he'd gone, to be sure.

Reconnoitring had always been one of my strong points. I was sure I'd be able to spot the men from a high vantage point. I glanced up to my right. I'd climb up there through the hazel bushes.

If they were making their way that two miles down towards the camp perimeter, I'd be able to spot them.

I got out of the car and locked it. No one was going to bother me. I just looked like a girl out for an afternoon walk. First, I walked along towards the car. I was so glad I'd worn my jeans and driving shoes. I was still stiff from the journey and tottered a little. All the time, as I was approaching the car, Richard's face kept rising before my eyes - that lovely smile, that handsome profile, *that injured leg. . .*

How could he trick people into thinking he was disabled? Anger made me hurry. I took a furtive look inside the Porsche. I'd been right. There was an empty camera case on the tiny back seat, along with maps and manuals, several newspapers and a rope. It didn't look a disabled driver's car. More like someone's who was used to the great outdoors. I looked up the bank. It was now or never.

A moment later, I was negotiating the deep ruts and a ditch full of scratchy ferns. The action of getting over jarred my bad leg. I tried to ignore the pain. It was absolutely necessary. . . I climbed to the top.

Using my hands, I caught at the hazel bushes and the brushwood, hauling myself slowly up the slope. Now I knew why the men had changed into boots. I had to stop several times for breath then, gritting my teeth against the pain, I carried on.

At the top, I almost collapsed, sprawling in the ferns. then I scrambled to my feet. I could hear my heart thumping in my ears. I was extremely unfit.

I was now looking from a high vantage point in the direction of the camp. How often I'd done this in the past, I thought. It was like second nature. I scanned the trees below, searching for a flash of colour in the greenery, for any movement. There was no sign of anyone.

I sat down. This gave me time to reflect on what I was doing. Was I being a fool? No, I'd been trained too well. The main problem was not being in the Army any more. I was an ordinary girl, sitting on top of a hill in the forest, playing at soldiers in the middle of nowhere.

Then, suddenly, I could see them, wriggling their way on another ridge about one hundred yards across the road. I prayed they wouldn't spot me. That made me think of the only thing that wasn't right. If they were up to no good, they would have been more careful about parking. That I didn't understand.

They'd stopped now and were passing the glasses from one to the other. They certainly weren't bird watchers. They were taking pictures of the terrain. If this had been an exercise and I'd been an officer, I would have shown myself and challenged them. I wasn't and this was for real. I despised Richard Main for whatever he was doing.

However, I had a marvellous description of them and their car. It was then I remembered I hadn't taken the registration number. What a fool. Just then, they wriggled off and disappeared. . . I'd just have to move back down very slowly if I was going to get that registration.

It was almost as hard coming down. I slipped and slid, hurting my hands and my bottom. And, of course, my leg. I had to sit and take a breather before I could sit up again.

As I neared the road, I could see they had got back before me. They were fit. They were talking animatedly, changing their boots, laughing. Richard's head was moving up and down as he stowed the gear.

I watched him from the cover of the bushes. . .

As soon as I heard the car doors slam and the engine rev up, I was on my feet and dashing, slipping and sliding down the slope to the road. But I was too late.

I reached the ditch as the car shot off. I ran out on to the road as it disappeared into the straight, but it was too far away for me to take the registration.

"You're losing your touch, Dean," I told myself sternly. "You're not the girl you were. Why didn't you get that number?"

There was one consolation. There couldn't be that many expensive sports cars of the same design in the area. Someone else would have seen it. It would be traced. All I had to do was pass on what I'd seen.

I struggled to my feet, dusting myself down. I had to get to a phone quickly, and I couldn't turn up at the camp like this, covered in mud. I'd go to the hotel and check in now, and change. Then I'd phone Tara. The hotel was only two miles away.

As I limped back to my car, I felt extremely miserable. I could hardly believe it. How could Richard Main be someone so devious? How could I have been taken in? It was too much. Could there be any other explanation?

Wearily, I unlocked the car, collapsed into the driver seat, switched on the ignition and drove out of the lay-by. As I spun power steering, I knew that I couldn't think of one single, convincing reason for his actions except the worst possible. Richard Main was up to no good.

CHAPTER 7

My leg ached as I waited at the hotel to be put through to Tara at the camp. I shifted uncomfortably from one foot to the other, then sat down on the comfortable chair by the bedroom window.

I'd stayed at *The Rainbow* before. It had been *after* a wedding that time - and it seemed the place to choose for an engagement party evening. It was also re-nowned for its good food, especially the trout, which had lent it its name.

My room had an excellent view. I could see across a sloping lawn, fringed with trees, above which the hills of Salisbury Plain stretched along the skyline. Through the half-open window, I could hear the noise of water from the stream that trickled on its way be-sides the hotel building into the lake and the fish farm behind the trees.

But, that day, I wasn't really taking-in the view. I had too much on my mind. I massaged my leg as I waited. Until that moment, I hadn't realised quite how much pain I was in after scrambling up that bank, nor how much the whole exercise had taken out of me. I was glad I'd abandoned my first plan, which had been to follow Richard. It would have been very silly indeed. Anything could have happened if they'd found they were being followed. No, I was more cautious than that these days. In fact, I was a lot less like the old, impulsive Alison.

"Come on, Tara, come on," I said impatiently. "Where the hell are you?"

The longer it took, the farther away the two men would be by now. I was desperate to pass on the information. Then I could relax.

I jumped. A series of clicks on the other end of the line confirmed I hadn't been cut off. I took the receiver away from my ear, then put it back quickly as I heard a man's voice.

"Hello, miss, sorry to keep you waiting but I'm afraid we can't find the sub-lieutenant at the moment. Will you try later, or is there a message?"

I breathed a sigh of frustration. I certainly didn't feel able to leave a message of that kind. I wanted to tell Tara personally.

"No, no message - except, should you see her, tell her Alison Dean will be with her as arranged."

"Right. Thank you, miss."

I put down the receiver, and went and lay on the bed, arms outstretched over my head, flexing my aching leg muscles as the hospital had taught me. I was all tensed up.

"Calm down," I told myself. "You've a good description of the men and the car, even though you were too thick to get the number."

I turned over in disgust, burying my head in the pillow. But I couldn't get Richard's face out of my mind.

I could hardly believe that the man I liked so much had been an impostor - and possibly a very dangerous one. It was then I wondered whether I should go directly to the police. But I didn't have any real evidence, only suspicions. And there was something inside which was telling me not to. . . Instead, I decided I'd run a bath.

Lying in it was a joy. The muscle cramps were beginning to ease away and making me feel human again. I felt even better as I sat in front of the mirror, but I knew I looked awfully pale.

But getting dressed for the party, and putting on my make-up made a real difference. I had taken a great deal of trouble, and it showed. My eye-liner made my eyes seem larger. The bronze eye-shadow was just the right shade and complemented my lipstick and blusher.

I looked good.

I stood up and turned this way and that. The top I had decided to wear was quite revealing but it suited me, showing off my slim arms and shoulders. I slipped on the cashmere cardigan casually and its soft warmth caressed my skin. I loved its expensive, elegant feel. The total effect appeared just right. Everything would have been just fine except for the persistent thought of Richard Main. How could he have tricked me like that? It was just so amazing how he'd turned up in the same place and at the same time as I had. I decided life was full of surprises and not always nice ones. But there had to be some meaning to it all.

I didn't even allow myself to think how lovely it would have been if Richard had been accompanying me to Tara's party. That was too painful and quite ironic that the one man with whom I appeared to have something in common, was a fake and might even be a terrorist. Unbelievable in fact. Slipping my key card into my small, brown-velvet evening-bag, I took a quick look at myself, checked I'd left nothing behind, and walked out of the hotel room, pulling the door to. I just couldn't wait to find Tara and tell her what I'd seen.

* * *

It was a strange feeling as I drove up to the gates of the camp. The soldier on the gates had evidently been alerted to the party and, after a cursory glance and a word with me, waved me through.

The camp was typical and just as I remembered. A conglomeration of huts and low brick buildings. Nothing picturesque, just functional. There seemed to be quite a lot of soldiers about for a weekend. But, whatever the day, they always had to be on guard. Security was tight all over the country and this camp, being so exposed, was no exception.

The man on the gate had given me directions, but Tara's party wasn't hard to find. I could see the white tent in the distance. On a lawned area behind the administration block.

I parked the car under the friendly eye of duty soldiers and, as I got out of the Escort, tried to hide my slight limp as I passed them. They didn't seem to notice because I caught their appreciative looks.

At the entrance to the marquee, I could hear the hum of voices. And then the band striking up. There were several people in front of me. As they moved on, I stepped inside. It was a delight. The place must have taken ages to decorate. In fact, I realised that Tara had jumped at the chance of using the camp's permanent marquee for her party.

I wouldn't have believed I was under canvas. The decor was quite spectacular. The inside of the enormous tent was quilted with white, silken material and festooned with decorations. There were even two chandeliers glittering at opposite ends. The tables were arranged in groups with six chairs around each one and at the end of the marquee, stood a long table where the buffet was laid out. The whole effect was marvellous.

Still it was a bit daunting being on one's own. But not for long. A young officer was by my side. He had very brown eyes and was extremely courteous.

"You're on your own?" He looked surprised.

I nodded and, at that moment, Tara rushed up to me, kissing me on both cheeks.

"You look lovely, Alison." She turned o the young man beside me. "Thanks, Dorian, I'll look after her now."

"Okay." I glimpsed disappointment in his eyes as Tara whirled me away.

"You really look great, Ally," she said as she piloted me across the marquee, nodding and smiling at everyone.

"So do you," I replied. Tara was a knock-out. She was wearing a full length slim dress in petrol-blue shot satin, which glimmered in the light from the chandeliers. It made her glow. "Where is *he*? I'm dying to meet him."

"Over there. Come on." There was such evident pride in her eyes that I felt a lump in my throat.

She was making for an officer who was giving instructions to the staff. Peter had the keen, piercing eyes of the professional soldier. Yet, as he smiled at me, I noticed they were kind and a vivid blue. He had dark hair and was tall. In fact, was an extremely good-looking guy. Tara had said he was older, but it wasn't noticeable.

Tara's face said it all as she introduced us - she was extremely proud of him.

The moment wasn't right for me to blurt out what I seen earlier. I would have to wait.

Tara and Peter must have invited the whole of the base. There were so many guests. I needn't have bothered about feeling conspicuous. I was surprised when I looked at my watch. In spite of all my fears, I had been chatting non-stop to lots of people I knew. The colonel, in particular, had seemed delighted to see me. He welcomed me as if I'd never been away.

"*Alison Dean*. How absolutely marvellous. Are you feeling better? We've missed you, you know."

"I've missed you all, but I'm doing fine."

"You're a brave girl," he said.

I wasn't sure if he was referring to the accident or to the fact I'd turned up at the party, but it made me feel better, although it was fairly embarrassing.

I was also chatted-up by Dorian Weeks, the guy who'd met me at the entrance. He was quite attractive, brown-haired, brown-eyed and with that peculiar clipped accent one develops after charging round Sandhurst. Evidently he had no idea I was

94

invalid ex-Army. It was a sticky moment when he asked me to dance, but the colonel turned up again at that moment and saved the day.

"Sorry, Dorian, Miss Dean has promised me the next - and the next, I'm afraid."

The young man must have got the message because his face went red and he disappeared quickly. I knew he wouldn't risk asking again, after being warned off.

The colonel chuckled. "Knew you weren't keen on dancing. Hope I haven't put my foot in it, Alison, but that lad's a bit bumptious. He's finding his feet. And he's also supposed to be on duty. I can't let him get away with it."

I laughed. Things hadn't changed.

I decided then to try to find Tara again. She had been very good, staying close until she was sure I was in conversation, then joining me now and again.

In spite of all her attention, I still felt depressed. I kept going over the afternoon's incident when I had seen Richard, trying to tell myself the two men were just innocently interested in the area around the camp. But I knew I had to do something about their behaviour.

I was thinking of going over to the buffet and joining the queue, where I spotted Tara standing in the middle of a small group of laughing friends. And then, my heart almost jumped into my throat.

I stared, telling myself I must be mistaken. But I knew I wasn't. The man who had just turned in my direction was nodding and smiling. It was none other than *Richard Main*. He hadn't noticed me in the crush. That wonderful smile was directed now at someone else - a high-ranking officer, whom I didn't recognise, *and* the colonel. He was shaking hands with both of them.

I stepped back on someone's foot, apologised hastily, and hurried towards the buffet queue. What was he doing here? I couldn't believe it. Was I going mad? Just who was he? What was his game? He wasn't in uniform. He couldn't be a soldier. Yet he appeared to know them all, and, once again, there was no sign of a stick or any disability.

He was disarmingly handsome and agile, his smartly-dressed frame, resplendent in dinner jacket and cummerbund, complementing the lithe, athletic build I'd admired so much.

I was out of breath as I pushed through the crowd. I must ask Tara who he was, and why she had invited him. I was trying to decide if I should even tell her about the afternoon incident as I struggled through the queue. I apologised to the group as I grasped her arm.

"Ally, what's up? Are you ill?"

Her friends had looked puzzled as she broke away. I felt annoyed at myself for making a scene. I shook my head.

"No, I'm sorry, Tara, but I have to ask you something. It's very important." I looked over to where Richard was standing. "Who's that?"

Tara looked, too, and grinned.

"To tell you the truth, I've no idea. But no wonder you're interested."

I was too upset to comment then that she shouldn't be looking at another man in that way at her engagement party.

"Do you want introducing?" she asked, but I shook my head.

"No. I have to speak to you. It's urgent."

She could see it was, and suddenly, her face became serious. We went and sat down. All the time I was wondering if Richard Main had seen me.

"Spill the beans then," Tara said. "What's the matter with the guy?"

"This might seem ridiculous, Tara, but I've seen him before. Today."

Tara stopped a passing waiter and took two glasses of wine.

"Go on then, but have a drink first. Slowly now. Plenty of time. Right?"

I leaned back against the chair and closed my eyes.

"Hold on," I heard her say.

I opened my eyes. Tara had caught hold of Peter, who was standing in front of us with two plates of food.

"Put those down, darling. I want you to hear what Alison's going to say."

He obeyed calmly.

"I rang you this afternoon . . ." I began.

"Yes, they told me in the office. I got the message."

"No, Tara, *you didn't*, at least not the message I wanted. You weren't around."

"I'm sorry Alison, I was busy."

I could see she had taken Peter's hand. Of course she wondered what was coming.

"Come on. What's happened? Please tell us."

"Do you remember when you came to see me in London, Tara, to invite me?"

I was watching Richard Main all the time, laughing and joking as if he hadn't a care in the world. I almost hated him for putting me through this. I swallowed.

"Do you know him, darling?" she asked Peter. "The guy over there with the colonel. And who's the major with him? Alison thinks she knows him.

I could see she wanted Peter to take over the questioning.

"I know the major. He's down here on some course but not the guy with him. Why? We did say everyone could bring a guest. What does Alison think the bloke's done?"

"I don't know."

It all came out in a rush then. I bit my lip, sorry I was spoiling their evening, but knowing, deep inside, that they would have been glad I still remembered what doing one's duty meant.

Peter was looking very serious as I told my story. "You mean the man over there is the same as the one you met in the Mall and you saw today taking shots of the camp?"

I nodded. I could see he was putting two and two together as would any good officer.

"And he was walking okay this time as well?" Peter said, watching him closely.

"Yes." I felt miserable enough to burst into tears.

"There was nothing wrong with him this afternoon? You're sure?" he repeated.

"Nothing. And I'm *quite* sure."

I was thinking about the expression of pain as Richard had slipped on the steps the day we met. *He must be the best actor in the world.*

"Right. Leave it to me. I'll pass it on, just in case. Well done, Alison. You haven't forgotten the drill."

But it was no time for self-congratulations. I hated the whole business. The party was spoiled for me. I couldn't bear to look in Richard Main's direction.

Peter walked off, and Tara and I watched him draw the colonel away from the group. They seemed to be talking for ages. It was then that Peter came back. I could see by his look he'd relaxed. We made room for him as he sat down. He was looking at the plates of food.

"Well, you might as well tuck in now," he said. "The heat's off."

"Darling, don't be so infuriating," Tara said. "Who is the man? I can tell you know by the look on your face."

"He's an actor, sweetheart."

"*An actor?*"

We sounded like a double act ourselves.

"Yes. He's the brother of the major in question, and is starring in some play which opens in the West End next week. His stage name is Dickon Maine. He's down here getting local colour. I wish I could earn my living like that. The new role's about a soldier, apparently, crippled in war, and trying to survive. So, Alison, he was having you on, I'm afraid. His acting must have been first-rate."

"It was," I said grimly, the force of my feelings almost overwhelming me.

An actor. Richard Main had conned me, and I'd fallen for his sob stuff. I was so angry. I'd been feeling sorry for him, identifying with him, and all the time, he'd been taking advantage.

Tara could see how upset I was. She was squeezing my hand sympathetically.

"Well, he's not a terrorist, which has to be good news."

I almost exploded then.

"Think what a fool I feel, Tara. Running after him and his friend, almost killing myself."

"Better than us being killed," Peter said seriously. "You did the right thing. And don't think about being made a fool of. That's his business, reflecting life as it is. He'll probably play the role superbly."

"Would you just go away, please?" Tara said. "Have you no tact? Can't you see this has made a fool of Alison?"

"Sorry," Peter said as Tara shook her head at him. I stood up.

"No, Alison, I'll go instead." Tara said when she realised where I was heading. "You stay with Peter, I'll go over to the buffet."

I walked off, planning how I could get away form the party as soon as possible. At that moment, someone touched my arm. I went rigid as I looked into Richard's eyes. They were showing surprise and delight.

"For goodness' sake, Alison. What are you doing here? What wonderful luck."

"I could ask you the same question. And I, personally, don't feel that lucky," I replied coldly, wanting him to hurt just as much as I did.

* * *

CHAPTER 8

Richard had an innocent look on his face, which I couldn't bear, given his deception.

"What do you mean?"

"I think you know, don't you?" I looked down sarcastically. "What happened to the stick? You've recovered, I take it? Was it painful?"

"Oh, I see. That." His face showed no trace of emotion. He appeared quite calm and matter-of-fact, as if he'd done nothing wrong.

"Yes, *that*," I snapped. "Now, if you'll excuse me, I don't think we've anything to say to each other."

I was so desperately disappointed at his reaction I turned away. What had I been expecting from him? Remorse?

But, all of a sudden, Richard was holding on to my arm, steering me towards the only quiet corner of the room. His grip was strong and all I could do, short of causing a scene, was allow him to escort me. Several people turned and smiled as we walked by. I could hardly acknowledge them, I was feeling so choked up inside.

"Let go," I said through my teeth, trying to speak quietly, and feeling anything but calm.

"You don't understand, Alison," he said. "Please, listen. I'm an actor. I was merely playing a part."

"Too right you were," I replied hotly now we were out of earshot of the other guests. "How could you pretend to use a stick, to be disabled, after all I told you about myself - my accident and everything." I wasn't making much sense. I could hear myself gabbling on while a sense of dark disappointment and hurt almost overwhelmed me.

"I see," he said. "That's it. I took you in, and you're angry. I'm sorry, but, believe me. I didn't mean to hurt you. I needed to get into the part. Evidently you see it differently."

"I do," I exploded, "because *I'm* not playing a part, Richard. And that's not even your name, is it?" I was angry with myself now for behaving so emotionally. "I'm living this every day," I went on. "How could you deceive me? It wasn't fair."

I was full of self-pity. He was silent. I moved away as he placed his hand on my arm and gave it a sympathetic squeeze.

"All right. It may seem like a rotten trick, I suppose, but, in the beginning, I had no idea what had happened to you. I had to test how good I was, whether or not my character was convincing. And you just happened to be standing there."

"Crying in the Mall," I said in disgust. "Fair game. But it wasn't right and you know it."

"I do now, and I'm sorry."

He had the nerve to smile, thinking that would make up. Once I'd thought he looked like Martin - now he was even behaving like him.

102

"Anyway, they say all's fair in love and war," he finished.

"Very funny," I replied. "This was neither."

He had a strange expression. I swallowed, trying to cover my confusion by attack. "You know you nearly ended up being arrested?" He arched his eyebrows.

"Yes," I went on. "I saw you this afternoon. In the forest. I thought you and your companion were some kind of terrorists, spying on the camp, and taking photos. I followed you."

To my utter annoyance, Richard began to laugh.

"Stop it," I said. "You could have been. What were you doing sneaking around anyway?"

"Doing a reccie. Getting into the character. Who knows? It was a stupid idea anyway. That's what I told the director, but he insisted. Now he's absolutely exhausted after the trek. He's not the athletic type."

Suddenly, Richard sounded as annoyed as I'd been. My initial, angry reaction was wearing off, probably I'd made him feel uncomfortable. At least, that gave me some satisfaction.

At that moment, I glimpsed Tara and Peter watching us.

"How dare you laugh?" I added furiously for effect. "If it wasn't for this being a party, I'd . . ."

"You'd what? Unmask me? Come on, please. Alison. Although it wasn't a very nice trick - I admit it, you see - it was necessary and, what's much better, it worked. I wanted it to. It had to, or it wouldn't have been authentic."

I stared him straight in the eyes. This man's arrogance had no bounds. And to think I had been weakening.

"I don't want to carry on this conversation one moment longer," I said suddenly. "I'm going."

But he was standing in front of me. "Please, Alison, don't. I'm really sorry. How can I make up?"

"You can't," I replied, hoping he wouldn't notice the tremor in my voice.

He looked quite magnificent when he was pleading. Then I realised it was all part of his charm. His looks were his assets. He was just one super-selfish ego. As I got up, he backed off, this time looking as if he was sorry.

"Do you always get as mad as this?" he said softly.

"When there's reason. Please let me pass."

"And you won't forgive me? Not even for art's sake."

"Not even for art," I said with bravado.

I mustn't let him see he was winning, but he was near to it. But I wasn't going to relent, not now. I wanted to teach him a lesson.

I was about to push past when an enthusiastic voice said, "Hello again, Miss Dean."

It was the young sub-lieutenant, Dorian, whom the colonel had dismissed. He'd evidently completed his duties. I smiled sweetly, noting with satisfaction the frown on Richard's face.

"Hello, there," I said. "As we missed out on our dance, why don't we go over to the bar for a drink?"

"Great."

The young officer took my arm.

I darted a glance at Richard, and said icily, "Goodbye. Nice to see you again."

And with that, I walked off. However, inside, I didn't feel any better. I knew that, if things had been right between us, I would much rather have been going for a drink at the bar with him. I wasn't being fair to Dorian either and, all round, I'd been behaving quite badly, even though Richard had thoroughly deserved it.

On the whole, I felt quite miserable over the next few hours. I shouldn't have been, because everyone treated me wonderfully and Dorian was exceptionally attentive.

However, now and again, I would glance across the room at Richard who always managed to look up at the same moment. As our eyes held each other's, I dropped my gaze. Dorian didn't seem to notice. It did me good to keep on talking and answering his questions about bookselling and military history.

"Gosh," he said, "I've always imagined what it must be like working in a bookshop. Reading all the time."

I thought of myself and Ralph rushed off our feet. He didn't know very much about bookselling, like most people.

But Dorian wasn't to be put off. "I've read a great deal about Napoleon," he insisted. "Admirable chap." Then I let him go on talking about the Battle of Borodino. It was just like old times. "I've enjoyed your company so much," he said as the evening drew to a close. "May I see you again?"

"I'm afraid I live in London," I hedged.

"Fine. I'm always up there on leave and at the weekends. Nothing like London for enjoying oneself. What about next Wednesday? We could take in a show, have dinner."

He only had to mention *show* and my mind was full of Richard - or Dickon - or whatever. It made me so angry to think of it.

"I'm not sure," I replied coolly. "We're very busy at work just now."

Dorian was a pleasant guy, but surely not for me. I knew that I shouldn't be allowing him to believe I liked him. I realised, too, what it was like being in the Army. When an male officer is on the move all the time, he always feels he needs stability in the shape of a regular girl friend, followed usually by marriage.

Suddenly, all I could think of was the idea of someone being Richard Main's wife. I told myself I was behaving quite ridiculously. I came back to the present with a jolt, trying to concentrate on what Dorian was saying. He looked extremely disappointed.

"Well may I phone you then? Perhaps we can fix something up soon."

I looked him in the eyes. I was just ready to tell him that I wasn't at all interested, when I saw Richard Main coming over. As he reached us and was about to speak, I smiled up at Dorian.

"Of course, I'll give you my number," I said. "I'm sure we can fix a date soon."

I hated myself for it, but I couldn't help it any more than Richard Main could help deceiving someone as vulnerable as I was. I pretended we'd only just noticed him, and I could see Dorian wasn't too pleased by Richard's appearance.

"Oh, hi," I said, my fingers resting lightly on Dorian's arm.

"I just came over to say goodbye. I've a lot to do."

Dorian was staring at him. I had to introduce them formally.

"Oh, goodbye then, Richard. Sorry, you two haven't been introduced, have you? Richard, this is Dorian, a friend of mine. Dorian, meet Richard. He's an actor, opening in a play about a soldier who's invalided out of the Army. He's down here to pick up some local colour. We met a short time ago."

I could see Dorian relaxing as soon as he realised by my tone Richard was just an acquaintance, not a rival. Dorian extended his hand, looking enthusiastic.

"An actor? I used to appear in our school plays regularly. Never was much good though."

Richard shook his hand briefly. "Well, mine's a bit beyond the school production, I think." He could be sarcastic too, evidently. And poor Dorian got the brunt of it. He looked down at me.

"Alison knows that," he added. "I'm a stickler for reality." He was looking me straight in the eyes. "Nice to meet you both." He nodded and walked off.

"Bit prickly, wasn't he?" Dorian said, frowning. "Still, these acting chaps have massive egos. Probably upset him by mentioning my thespian activities at school. Now, Alison, where were we?"

He put out his hand and took mine. As he did, Richard turned on his heel and walked out the room. He'd got the message.

It was all my own fault, of course. However, somewhere inside, a little voice was saying, "You've done it now, you stubborn fool. Serve you right. He's proud. He's walked out of your life."

But that was what I wanted, wasn't it? I'd probably never see him again. . .

In spite of what I felt, it was nice to have someone to talk to, someone who was interested in me. Dorian was certainly that. He reminded me of so many of the eager young men I'd trained with and whom I'd never encouraged because I'd thought I'd fallen for Martin. I told myself that I wasn't a very good judge of men as he explained in an animated way what he wanted from his career in the Army.

By the look of him, I fancied he'd never make higher than Captain, but I suppose that was a bit nasty of me. Dorian had ingenuous brown eyes under fine brows and appeared to be following everything I said with interest. Here was someone who would never think of pulling a stunt like Richard Main. Indeed, I doubted whether Dorian had the imagination. But that was nasty too. It was amazing that every guy I truly wanted was totally unsuitable. Now, here I was again with another, Dorian, who was good company and appeared to like me, but I wasn't keen on him.

Suddenly, those familiar feelings of self-pity were welling up and, to my horror, tears stung behind my eyes. I'd never been a cry baby, but it was a trait I was developing fast. I was disgusted with myself. I stared into my drink, hoping to cover my ridiculous distress but Dorian, nice guy that he was, had noticed.

"You look upset," he said. "I imagine this has been an ordeal for you. I hope you don't mind me mentioning this but . . . I spoke to Tara, and she said you'd been in the Army and . . ."

I could see he couldn't handle it. "It doesn't matter," I said. "I'm over it now." I was an accomplished liar.

"It must have been so dreadful for you. Do you feel any better now and - I'm awfully sorry about . . ." he was swallowing under his tight uniform collar, ". . . about asking you . . ."

"To dance?" I finished the sentence for him. "No, don't be embarrassed, Dorian, there are lots of things worse than having a leg injury." I must have sounded so convincing that Dorian immediately agreed with me. He was a typical man, not at all diplomatic.

"Yes, I suppose there are. I knew a bloke who was in the Falklands and had both his legs blown off."

"Really," I said. Then Dorian went red. I put out my hand and touched his arm. "Don't let's talk about it." He nodded. I drained my glass, "You know, I could do with another drink."

I've never seen anyone move so quickly. It was then I caught Tara's eye. I smiled and she replied with a wink. She thought I was having a good time.

After I had said my goodbyes, Dorian and I left the base together. I knew he was hoping I'd come in a cab but, when he knew I had my own car he walked me to it.

"Would you mind terribly if I followed you and we had a goodnight drink at your hotel?" As I looked into those honest brown eyes, I knew that Dorian wasn't that wet behind the ears.

"I don't know if that would be a very good idea," I said. "I have to drive back to London early in the morning."

"But it's not that late, and I'm off duty." His tone was pleading.

I laughed. I knew what it was like trying to get away, trying to be a normal bloke instead of taking orders all the time.

"Okay then," I replied.

The young officer looked very happy indeed. All the way back to the hotel, I could see his headlights close behind me and all the time I was telling myself off for not being straight with him. I wasn't interested in Dorian Weeks at all. He was just someone who was there when I needed comforting.

"Alison," I said to myself, "you're really mixed-up, aren't you? You know who you do want and it just isn't possible." I couldn't fall for another deceiver. And Richard Main was one.

I waited for Dorian to swing round into the parking space beside my car. He jumped out efficiently and came round to my side and opened the door. As I got out, Dorian slipped his arm under mine and we walked into the hotel together.

As the night porter handed me my key, I said, "Is the bar still open?"

"Sorry, miss, we closed at eleven. But I can get you something sent up." His face was quite expressionless.

"Well," I said, "I don't know. Umm . . . what do you think, Dorian?" I was placing the ball squarely in his court.

"I think we should have a night-cap before I go home," he said.

The porter's expression didn't change. "Certainly, sir, what can I get you?" His eyes flicked over Dorian's uniform which was unmistakable.

He really should have gone home to change as, usually, it isn't wise to let everyone and anyone know you're a soldier. And a porter this close to the camp would know so.

110

"Alison?" asked Dorian.

I looked at him steadily. "Gin and tonic?" Not a good night-cap really but I needed it. Having had to drive, I'd restricted myself all evening to a couple of small glasses of wine; now I felt stone cold sober and needed a drink to calm my nerves. I was behaving foolishly but I also needed Dorian's company.

"Great. And whisky for me."

"I'll bring it up, sir." The porter was already crossing the hall as we, two, went upstairs. . .

Dorian took the tray from the man and closed the door. Meanwhile, I'd unfastened the window on to the summer night and was standing there to clear my head. Down below, the small trout stream trickled on and the scent of roses came up from the garden. It had been raining again which had made those night smells even more fragrant.

I thought how romantic it would have been with the right man. . . Dorian was coming over with two glasses in his hand. We stood by the heavy drapes and looked out into the darkness.

"Nice room," he said.

"Dorian . . . I . . . I don't want you getting the wrong idea." It was a mean thing to say. And unsophisticated. Of course he had the wrong idea. What bloke wouldn't being invited up to a hotel room at nearly midnight?

"I shan't," he said. "It's nice . . . just being with you. Frankly, I don't get much time for things like this," he swallowed a gulp of whisky.

That wasn't a chat line. It was just so true. When did an officer have time to make any real contact with a woman? Not very often in my experience.

111

"That's not to say I don't miss it," he added. He was very close as he said the last sentence. "I did say a *drink*, Alison. And I don't think the colonel would be too happy if he saw me now."

"The colonel. Whatever do you mean?"

"He got rid of me as quickly as he could, didn't he? I'm not his blue-eyed boy at the moment."

"Why? What have you done?"

"I don't know. I think he sees me as a bumptious brat."

I grinned. I couldn't help it; Dorian looked so young and forlorn, whereas that uniform should have made him Action Man. I could see also he wasn't that used to picking up women.

"Well, *I* don't think so."

"You don't?" Now he looked extremely happy.

"Not at all. You're a very nice guy."

"Thank you."

I finished the gin and went and sat down on the couch. He followed me, sat down too and next moment he had his arm round me. I looked into those big brown eyes.

"Do you want me to take my arm away?"

"As long as it *stays there*," I said, "it'll be all right."

He took the hint. We sat chatting for a while and, once or twice, I thought if he hadn't been such a nice guy I might have ended up in bed with him. Sometimes I had no sense. But that wouldn't have been fair because I knew I was going to drop him soon.

He did kiss me though. He had gentle undemanding lips, which made me know even more he wasn't used to women. I didn't respond and, after that, he removed his arm. We talked a lot more about the Army and what had happened to me.

I even told him about Martin which was uncharacteristic. Evidently telling Richard Main over dinner that night had opened the floodgates and something which had been keeping me back from telling anyone was now unleashed. I wanted to wish I hadn't told Richard but I couldn't because, however angry I was with him and his play acting, I'd had a magical time. . .

Dorian looked at me, "Well, I know I'm boring but you look as though you're awfully tired."

"Oh, sorry," I said, collecting my thoughts, "it's been a long day. Nice though." I was becoming an excellent liar.

"Thanks." He got up reluctantly and pecked me on the cheek. "I reckon I should go now and leave you to have a good sleep. But that doesn't mean I wouldn't like to see you again. Will you let me, Alison? When I'm in London on Wednesday?"

I should have told him there and then, but I hadn't the bottle. Instead, I answered, "Yes, I think Wednesday's okay."

He looked delighted. We walked over to the door together and Dorian opened it. I knew he was going to kiss me again before he left. Next moment he had his arms round me and his lips pressed against mine. It was only when we heard the footsteps in the corridor that we broke apart. . .

I couldn't believe it when I saw the man walk past me, his familiar hair, deep blond in the muted light of the corridor. *Richard again.* He walked along and pressed his key card into the lock of a door about five away from mine. He didn't look at either of us. I watched him over Dorian's shoulder. He went in and shut the door.

Dorian seemed oblivious as he straightened his tunic. "Well, thanks, Alison, it was super." His voice seemed extra loud and eager. "I'll ring you soon."

"Right," I said and I knew my voice was shaky. There was no chance he hadn't recognised me.

"Goodbye, then," said Dorian, regretfully lingering.

"Bye, I have to go," I said, stepping back into my room and shutting the door on him gratefully. Then I hurried over to my bed and flung myself down. How could Richard have been staying in the same hotel and on the same corridor? I couldn't bear it. It was just my luck. I'd been right earlier. I wasn't lucky to-night.

I assumed I knew what he was thinking as well: that I was the kind of person who went to bed with any soldier who showed the slightest interest in me. *I couldn't bear it. It just wasn't fair.*

I went straight to sleep, but I was plagued with horrible dreams - a mixture of all kinds of fears, like racing through the rainy dark and finding myself lying trapped under the car. Worst of all, as I saw them pulling Martin from the wreckage, I was looking not into his vacant eyes and broken face but into Richard Main's. . . Then my dreams turned to violent acts, to terrorists, to every worst nightmare in the world and every night ghost's face was Richard's. . .

I felt exhausted and stiff when I woke out of my uneasy dreams the following morning. Lying there

114

in the already warm summer light, trying to relax, I went over and over the events of the night before.

It was no good. I'd assured Tara and Peter that I'd had a great time at their party. It had been partially the truth, but my encounters outside and inside the camp with Richard Main had been both alarming and surprising, while my last, in the corridor, had beaten them all as total embarrassment.

I knew I cared what the actor thought about me, in spite of telling myself I didn't, I probably would never seen him again now. But, at least, he wasn't a terrorist, which would have been the worst of all.

The sound of the phone made me jump. I wasn't expecting a call. What had gone wrong? It was only seven a.m. on Monday, for heaven's sake.

"Good-morning." The cheerful voice belonged to Dorian Weeks, and he sounded as if he hadn't a care in the world. "Sleep well?"

"Fine," I lied, as I thought of those horribly vivid nightmares - Martin, Richard, the accident, all jumbled together in my consciousness.

"So what about our date then?" I hesitated at the pleading tone. I didn't really want to see Dorian again. "Oh, sorry." He was extremely apologetic. "Have I rung too early? Forgive me. Shall I phone later?" He was smitten. I could tell.

I sighed. "No, no. I'll be off home straight after breakfast. Give me a ring at the shop tomorrow."

I'd given him Ralph's number and I was already regretting it. I knew I'd really put my foot in it with him. He'd sounded so keen when we'd said goodbye.

At about eight-thirty, I looked in the mirror and shook my head at my reflection.

"Alison Dean, you're a prize idiot. You know there's only one man you want to phone you. Whatever he's done, you're hooked on him."

I'd thought it through and it was true. This wasn't like Martin over again. This was different. For me anyway. Whether it was for him, I didn't know.

Anyway, I'd done it. I'd scared him off. I knew he wasn't a man to be snubbed. It was probably true I wouldn't see Richard again.

When I went down to breakfast, I wasn't in a good mood. It had all been too much for me, I concluded. And I was dreading the thought he might be sitting at the table opposite.

As I walked into the dining room, I was feeling very nervous. What could I say? Should I just ignore him or brave it out? After all, it wasn't his business who I slept with. And I certainly hadn't slept with Dorian. But how did Richard know that? He'd gone into his room while we were kissing.

I expect he thought we'd spent the night together. What else would he think when he saw us kissing with the door open? It was an awful situation. I breathed in deeply and looked round. There were several people eating, but no Richard.

I was on tenterhooks as I ordered. He might walk in any minute. I assumed I looked pale when the waitress said, "Did you have a good night, miss?"

"Wonderful."

"Coffee or tea?"

"Coffee, please, and make it black." I needed to come

to my senses. And I had to drive all the way to London feeling like this. . .

Thankfully, Richard Main didn't turn up and, when I was stowing my case outside in the car park there was no sign of his black Porsche either. He must have made an early start.

* * *

CHAPTER 9

As I pulled out of the Rainbow's car park, I decided to go home a different way. I didn't want to pass the camp, so I would have to take another road. Neither did I feel like passing the spot where I'd followed Richard Main and his companion either. I realised it was silly of me, but that was how I felt that Monday morning.

Once more, I couldn't help thinking of all that had happened last night; seeing so many familiar faces again which, however much I tried, brought back hurtful memories and, on top of that, my disappointment at the Richard Main episode, a meeting which could have otherwise been magical.

The road took me through several pretty villages lying on the edge of Salisbury Plain. There were lots of bends veering crazily which a driver, who didn't know the road and going fast, could have misjudged altogether and ended up in a ditch.

But I found I was remembering this narrow road really clearly as I drove along. Later, I had to jam on the brakes to avoid a slow-moving tractor that had pulled out from a concealed gateway. The driver seemed half-asleep, his vehicle throwing up a mud-storm from beneath the huge tyres. There was no opportunity to pass at all, so I settled down, remembering that about a mile on there was a long stretch of dual carriageway. It was difficult to be patient though, not to try to overtake; that would have been crazy.

The road was even narrower now, bordered on one side by feathery rushes fringing a little stream that meandered all the way to Salisbury; the same stream which crossed through the Rainbow Hotel's grounds.

I was just thinking absent-mindedly what a slow journey this was turning out to be, when the tractor driver applied his brakes hard. I almost went into the back of him.

Shocked, I saw him turn in his seat, making gestures for me to reverse. There was no-one behind but I felt cross. Then I realised there must be something ahead which was bigger, which he knew had the right of way.

Looking in the mirror, I reversed and he followed. Suddenly, there were more cars coming behind, and I had to stop. The tractor pulled right into the ditch. As he moved, I could see why.

There was a column of army transporters approaching, their lights blazing, behaving like they owned the road. As I squeezed myself into the verge, I remembered how I'd felt riding in one. As if the traffic was nothing; as if no one could touch me. Powerful.

They were breaking rules taking this short cut though. They were meant to stay on the major road although it was the long way round to the camp. But they didn't care. They were bigger than most on the road. And they were in a hurry.

I sat while they thundered past like great, green-painted whales. the first trucks were full of soldiers in camouflage, who stared hard at the occupants of the cars below them. Several were grinning.

The lorries were followed by two jeeps. I pressed on the clutch, ready to move, as the tractor began to crawl out of the ditch. Could I accelerate past him? Had I the cheek as the second jeep approached?

As I was deciding, I revved up and, accidentally, let my foot off the clutch, stalling my engine as the jeep and I were parallel. I gasped.

It was driven by a sergeant, and beside him was seated a fair-headed, young officer, who was holding an orthopaedic stick in his hand. Richard Main. *The man was everywhere - and still playing a part, getting into the character*, as he called it.

Our eyes met. He grinned too, then lifted the stick slightly as if in salute. I sat numbly, ignored him, biting my lip. Suddenly, horns were honking, telling me to get a move on. Coming to, I restarted the car and caught up with the crawling tractor ahead.

That smile of Richard's had hit me like a sniper's bullet. I knew it was Fate. I'd probably keep on meeting him, and our accidental relationship would continue to develop as a series of awful misunderstandings.

I was very glad when I reached the dual carriageway at last. It gave me the chance to accelerate and clear my mind as to what course I should take.

Soon, Wiltshire was far behind me, but Richard's

120

face stayed with me. You can imagine my thoughts as the car ate up the miles towards London, where the whole strange business had begun. Tomorrow, I would be back in that tiny bookshop in Shaftesbury Avenue where Ralph was waiting patiently, not only for the news of my weekend adventures, but for the worst bookshop assistant he'd ever had the misfortune to employ. My head was aching all the way home.

* * *

I hurried into the shop out of breath one minute after opening time on Tuesday. I'd meant to be earlier but there had been a security alert on the Underground.

"Well, you don't look too happy," Ralph said.

Neither did he. He took off his spectacles and cleaned them on his cardigan. I knew he had something on his mind. Then he put up his hand and rubbed tired eyes.

"And there was I thinking a change would do you good. That you might meet someone to cheer you up."

"It did - it did," I half-lied, trying vainly not to go over the whole fiasco again. "I had a super time."

How could I tell Ralph my visit to Salisbury had been worse than a mistake, more like a catastrophe? Then Dorian's eager face rose in my mind. The sub-lieutenant would have to come to my rescue again.

"I managed to get a date though," I volunteered brightly.

"That must be a start," Ralph replied, putting on his glasses and looking more cheerful. "Doubtless your mother will be delighted. Army?"

"Yes, and I haven't told her. And I shan't. There's nothing to tell."

Both Ralph and my parents knew I'd said I'd never go out with someone from the Army again.

"Really? Well, I get the message," my cousin replied. "Don't worry, your secret's safe with me. When's the date?"

"I've no idea. He said he'd ring. His name's Dorian."

Suddenly, Ralph was looking extremely irritable. He picked up a venerable-looking copy of the Old Testament and stared at it fixedly. I waited.

"Humph! Dorian, eh? Humph!" His tone was grumpy, and he was usually so good-tempered. I'd evidently upset him. "Dating can't be what it was in my day. If you don't know *when*, how can you be going out with him? Funny behaviour."

I knew the danger signs. Ralph was the sweetest man but, at that moment, I realised that it would be diplomatic to get on with my work and shut up. Sometimes, he was just as old-fashioned as Mother.

I glanced at the children's books waiting to be shelved and began to put them away very quickly, puzzled as to why he'd taken an instant dislike to my mention of Dorian. . .

* * *

"You can stop doing that now," Ralph said later. "Why don't you go and make us both a coffee?"

I could see he was getting over whatever it was that was bugging him.

"All right."

I put down the books I was holding and walked through into the kitchen. I gasped at what I saw, turned - and Ralph was right behind me.

"Well?" He shook his head. "What do you think of that?"

What could I think? There was an enormous spray of flowers lying on the sink unit.

"And his name isn't Dorian," Ralph said. "I just wish you'd sort out your men."

He handed me the card which had come with the flowers. There were about twenty red roses and just as many carnations. On the work top stood another massive bouquet of Singapore orchids, which lit the back room with their purple and orange fire.

I held the card with trembling fingers. It was gilt-edged, with two golden masks in the corner, one smiling, one tragic. I swallowed as I read the message.

From the man with two faces. Forgive me? Dickon.

"When did they come?" I asked.

"Yesterday afternoon. Doubtless, the young chap thought you'd be at work on Monday. You're keen on the D's, aren't you Alison?"

"Some of them." My face was red-hot.

"This one must be special, I should think," Ralph said. "He must have spent a fortune. I wonder what your mother would say about this?"

"I don't know, but I'm not going to tell her."

"Neither am I. That's the beauty of a male cousin. He minds his own business. Where are you going to put them though?"

I laughed out loud. "I'll find somewhere. He's an actor, you know - not Dorian. This other one."

How could I explain? I felt I had to give some kind of explanation. "And you've met him."

"I have?"

"Yes. He's the one with the stick."

Ralph frowned. "That one?"

"Yes, and he was only pretending. This is to make up."

I knew Richard had succeeded, because my heart was giving nervous, little jumps. I was going to see him again - that was all that seemed to matter.

"A bit flamboyant, eh? Fits with the image, I suppose. Where's he performing?" Ralph was showing a most unusual interest in it all.

"It's a long story, Ralph," I said, trying to calm down.

"And just where does this Dorian fit in?"

I could see Ralph was determined to hear the whole thing. Just then, the phone rang beside me, making us both jump. I picked it up. "Ralph's Books!"

My head whirled at the eager voice I heard. "When can we meet, Alison? I'll be up in London on Wednesday at the Officer's Club. Please, don't say no."

I couldn't keep on using Dorian like this. I'd have to tell him.

"All right. Wednesday then. But I'd rather it be just a drink. . . Yes, you can pick me up. . . Ralph's Books, opposite Mancini's."

When he hung up, Ralph's eyes were glinting. "Which one was that?"

"Dorian, I'm afraid. But I don't think it'll last."

He laughed. "Alison Dean, if I'd known you were counting on playing games like this, I'd never have employed you. For goodness' sake, make the coffee. I hope you know what you're doing."

I hoped I did, too, but my heart was leaping about again. Just as I was pouring out, Ralph clutched at his breast pocket.

"Dear me, I almost forgot. This came for you, too."

It was a plain envelope, except for my name. I opened it carefully, withdrawing a theatre ticket. It was for a front seat, in the stalls, for the new play "Adversity," starring Dickon Maine. I showed Ralph.

"Ah, Dickon Maine. Yes. It's on up the road. Excellent previews, too. I come past every day. Seems your friend is quite excellent in the role."

It was true. I hadn't seen the previews but I'd passed it, too, on my way to the shop. Recently. Since it had been advertised. I usually ignored publicity pictures.

No way was I going to see anything about a play in which a soldier becomes crippled for life. If only I'd known before Richard was the star, things would have been a lot less complicated. I stared at the ticket. I'd have to go, otherwise I'd never know what made Dickon tick.

I looked up, to see Ralph looking at me closely.

"I can see by your face that you'll be going," he said. "And I've also got the feeling that Dorian has lost his first battle. Now I can tell you what Dickon said."

"You've seen him?" I could feel the excitement inside.

"Yes, Alison. He brought in the flowers personally last night before I closed up. . ."

"Well, go on," I urged, desperate to hear what Richard had said.

"You remember last week, when I got on my high horse and gave you a talking to? . . . Well, there's

125

another one coming. I've no right, of course, but I do like to see justice done. I think that bloke is all right. He told me the lot, how you thought he'd been having you on, about him using a walking-stick, and why. He asked me to say a few words on his behalf."

"Did he?" I was more than surprised. Richard didn't seem like that kind of guy. He seemed able to fight his own battles, and to think I had thought I'd never see him again.

"I can see by your face you don't think much of that, Alison, but as a man, I can tell you how much it means. It takes guts to ask another man to help you, if you're smitten."

"Smitten?" I asked incredulously.

"Yes, I could see the bloke was crazy about you. Take it from me."

"Crazy about me?" I echoed.

"Crazy enough. I've seen that look in a lad's eyes before. Poor devil."

I burst into laughter. "Oh, Ralph. You're so funny."

"No, that's a women's prerogative. Now are you going to keep that young fellow dangling, just because he upset you? How was he to know you'd a big chip on your shoulder? He told me he'd been walking round on sticks for six months in preparation for his role. That's dedication for you.

"Yes, that's a man to be reckoned with. And I don't see him as being patient for ever. If you want him, I suggest you get down to the theatre on Thursday. . . By the way, he said would you come round to his dressing-room after the performance. . . An offer no woman could refuse."

Ralph's eyes were twinkling. I'd never imagined him as a go-between before, but he was making a thorough job of it.

"Well, Ralph, I never thought you were like my mother, but I know better now, don't I? You don't pull your punches. I will go because I like him better than anyone I've ever met. Will that do you?"

"And that phone call?"

"I'll tell Dorian when I see him that I've made a mistake. I'm sure he won't be too unhappy."

"Good girl," Ralph said.

Whatever Dickon had said to my cousin, it had made an enormous impression. . .

* * *

When we met, Dorian took it all quite well. He turned his glass round in his hand, inspecting it carefully.

"I had the feeling. Don't apologise. I could see there was something between you and that other chap. But I had to have a go. Male ego, I suppose. Shan't be going to see the play, though. Too near the mark for my liking."

I was surprised to hear that it had been obvious how I felt about Richard - I could never get use to calling him Dickon.

Dorian put his glass down on the table and looked at his watch. "I'll have to be making tracks, Alison," he said. "Duty calls. Now, shall I get you a cab?"

Dorian kissed me on both cheeks when we parted. I should have felt ashamed about using him, but he didn't seem to mind. However, I knew he'd soon have another female in tow. He was the eager kind, and most girls love a uniform.

I leaned back in the taxi as it nosed its was through the evening traffic. As it crawled along Shaftesbury Avenue, I allowed myself to look at the theatre hoardings.

It was so strange to read Dickon's name, and to see the look on his face, pale and haunting, peering from the enormous photographs outside the theatre. It was a tragic face, twisted with pain, the face I first remembered when I met him after the rainy meeting on Saturday in the Mall.

It was then that I remembered the little masks on his card and knew that happiness always went hand-in-hand with tragedy, and that Fate had taken a hand in making Alison Dean part of real life once more.

* * *

CHAPTER 10

It had been a long time since I'd visited the theatre and, certainly, on my own. My parents often asked me to go with them, but the thought of sitting two hours, with only an interval to stretch my bad leg, had put me off. Tonight, stiffness or not, I was determined to be there. The West End stage has its own particular magic, and I could feel it as soon as I stepped through the heavy glass doors.

I'd already spent a few minutes outside, staring at the huge photo of Dickon Maine, whose morose expression and gloomy eyes were very far removed from the Richard I knew. Inside, I felt a glow of pride, almost as if he belonged to me already. But I still wasn't sure about anything.

Maybe he'd sent the flowers and the tickets out of a sense of duty. Because of the upset he'd caused me? But he'd asked Ralph to plead on his behalf. That was really strange; and quite sweet.

Inside the foyer, there were more photographs, which appeared to establish Dickon as the season's brightest new star. He'd had excellent notices. Dickon was famous already and, a feeling inside, told me that he'd be even more so when the run ended. It was then I wondered what it would really be like to be a top class actor. Never being oneself; always somebody else.

The crowds of people around me milled about looking for friends or acquaintances, buying or collecting tickets. I pulled mine out of my small sequinned black evening bag. I hoped I looked all right. After all, he had invited me round to his dressing room after the show. I'd never experienced such an invitation before and, once again, I'd found it difficult to decide what to wear. I wanted to create the right impression.

So I'd put on a long flowing skirt and silk shirt. The jacket I wore on top had been very expensive. I'd secured it in the Dickins & Jones sale and, every time I wore it, I felt good. As I moved across the foyer and handed in my ticket to the usher, my heart was beating very fast. Then I was walking through the red, velvet curtains into the front stalls.

The atmosphere was buzzing with conversation and excitement and I must have been the most excited girl in the audience. It was a thrilling experience knowing the leading man had invited me personally; that he wanted *me* to be there. I looked round at the glittering tiers of seats and thought again what it would be like playing to a full house. I was even more excited when the fire curtain lifted to reveal heavy red velvet drapes fringed with golden tassels. The front seat was very comfortable. There was plenty of leg room and it was then I realised Richard must have picked the seat which would have suited me most.

When the curtain finally went up, I couldn't wait to see him and, from then on, I was transported into another world. And it was a world I knew. I was back in the Army again, reliving every moment I'd prized, and happy that I hadn't been called on to face the terrible battle the hero had.

And he was a hero. He wasn't the Richard Main I knew. He was just a wounded soldier, with whom I could identify. It was marvellous tear-jerking performance. Yes, sitting in the darkness of that London theatre I was crying again.

I could see now why Richard had worked so hard at pretending for six months. It had paid off. It seemed like he hadn't been pretending at all. This was why Dickon Maine was a great actor.

I rummaged in my bag for a handkerchief, remembering when Richard had first lent me his. It had come to a part in the play where Captain Cavan Mahoney, the hero, had been airlifted to hospital and told it was unlikely he would ever walk again. If I hadn't cared about Richard so much, I wouldn't have been able to sit through the play. It brought back too many memories. And. here I was, crying like a silly, emotional fool.

When the lights went up for the interval, I was extremely conscious that my face was streaked with tears. I got up, winced as my bad leg stiffened and made for the powder-room as quickly as I could, afraid my mascara had run down my cheeks. It had, but only a little. Yet I wasn't the only one; other women had been crying too.

When I came out, I couldn't face pushing my way through to the bar area as there was such a crush. Instead, I returned to my seat - to find an usherette waiting with coffee on a tray and a beautifully-wrapped small box of fine Belgian chocolates.

"Dickon Maine sent these with his compliments and asked me to remind you to come backstage afterwards," she said.

"Thank you so much. Please tell him I haven't forgotten." I was overwhelmed, and felt so very special. He must have forgiven my nastiness to him at the camp. In my heart, I knew he'd forgiven me everything. I undid the box, popped a beautiful truffle into my mouth and sat there, staring at the stage, hardly able to wait for curtain up.

The second act turned out to be a revelation. Everything that Cavan Mahoney had to face was familiar to me. The play could have been written with me in mind. It was uncanny. Even *I* felt the hero would never get to grips with his terrible disability.

There was a point in the script which was almost identical to our experience in the Mall, where the hero meets a girl, whose bravery in her own adversity helps him to get on his feet again.

After that, I took more and more notice. It was like going through my own life with a narrator. I found myself waiting for the high point, desperate to know how Cavan copes in the end, how it was all going to turn out.

I wasn't to be disappointed. Cavan won his girl finally and found out he could face life. Tears were running down my face as they embraced - and it wasn't until the next scene I thought about Richard holding that very attractive leading lady in his arms and kissing her so realistically. I concluded that's what you had to put up with, if you had an actor for a boy friend.

But it was excellent theatre, and all due to the brilliant acting of Dickon Maine. I was sure this play would run for a very long time. I clapped frantically as he returned for the fourth curtain call. The reception he was getting brought another lump to my throat I was so proud of him I wanted to yell, "*I know him. He's my boy friend.*" But he wasn't . . . yet.

When I was shown to his dressing-room. I hardly recognised him. He looked exhausted, weary from the battle he'd been fighting. His face was sombre and he was just putting a pair of crutches behind the door when he answered my knock. The crutches fell over immediately.

"Damn things," he said, turning to retrieve them.

"Don't call them that," I stooped and picked them up. We almost knocked heads.

We came up together and I stared him in the eyes. There was a moment's silence and then the words were rushing out. "Those crutches did you a service. You were absolutely fantastic, Richard. It was out of this world. It'll run for ever. What more can I say?" My pent-up excitement at his performance burst out.

He was smiling, but he looked sad too. "You enjoyed the play then? I'm glad, Alison. Really glad. Would you like to sit down? There isn't much room."

He cleared the dress uniform and sword he'd worn in the first act off the chair. It was then I realised how well made-up he was. I knew I was staring.

"Off with the greasepaint, Alison Dean, and back to reality. Give me a moment."

I was fascinated. "Do you have to do that all the time?"

"Yes, it's a necessary bore." He began to look more normal, in fact, as ordinary as the man I'd met for the first time in the Mall.

"It was a full house. And they were crying at the end," I said, sitting down to watch.

He didn't answer. He was looking at me in the mirror, the same vulnerable look which I'd thought was just part of his charm. Now I knew better. It was him and part of his talent. I sensed he was remembering that rainy afternoon, too.

"I'm sorry I'm a bit quiet," he said, "but it's always like this. You have to get out of the part as much as in." I nodded. "Do you understand?"

"Yes, I do, but what I don't understand is how you can do that every night."

"Do what?"

"*Be* Cavan Mahoney. It must drain you totally."

"It does, believe me. You have to shake yourself out of it and then do it all over again tomorrow. And if there's a matinee . . ."

I shook my head at the thought. "I suppose I never realised quite how difficult it is to act."

"No . . . but you're not a bad actor yourself."

I blushed. "Is that meant to be a compliment?"

"Yes. You know, I'd never have guessed you were disabled either."

"Wouldn't you, Richard? . . . I mean . . . Dickon."

"Richard'll do. . . . I didn't think you'd come, you know." He had taken off his make up and was swivelling towards me in his chair. He took both my hands in his.

"Why not?"

"I thought it might be too painful. The story, I mean. Believe me, Alison, there was no way I was using you as research. You do believe me, don't you?"

"Yes. And I came because of you. I have to confess I didn't know anything about the play. But it was a revelation. The way you played it as if you knew how it felt."

"That's my job. I could never be as brave as you."

"As brave as me?" I was amazed. "I'm not brave. If only you knew about all the self-pity, all the times . . ."

He put a finger to my lips. "Shush. You are brave and you came, Alison, and that's all that mattered."

My heart was beating very fast. "Thank you for the flowers and for inviting me." I was so confused I didn't know what else to say. "Oh, and the coffee and chocs. I didn't expect any of it."

"I'm glad you liked them. I hoped you would." He got up from his chair at the same moment I did. Then his arms were round me. They felt warm and strong. I just savoured that wonderful moment. "I'm glad you came. It wouldn't have worked if you hadn't been there."

"I don't understand." I was looking into those honest eyes.

"I mean the play tonight was all for you, Alison."

I shook my head. "No. It was for everyone. It was wonderful."

"But I wanted it to mean most to you, because . . ."

I could see him hesitate. I realised he was going to say something which was difficult to explain.

"Yes?"

135

". . . because you were the one who sparked it off, made it live. Before, it was just words that I had to bring to life, like all actors do. But I found the real words through you. After meeting you, talking to you, feeling your pain with you. . ."

"Stop. Please, I don't want to hear." It was all too much. "You hardly know me."

"I can't stop, and I want to know you, everything about you. And, if this play continues to be a success, it's because *you're* a success. I'm sorry if you thought I was using you. I wasn't. I wanted to make people know what it's really like to have to give up something, someone you love, through no fault of your own. If I've done that, then I've succeeded." He breathed in deeply.

"You mean so much to me, Alison. I was trying to get to grips with the script that day we met. I'd almost given up on trying to play Mahoney because, you know I've never suffered. I've got off lightly. Maybe I've been broke, but I've never had to put up with what you've had to. Thank you, Alison. Thank you for the play, for everything."

"No-one else but you could have said that." I sniffed, rummaging stupidly for my handkerchief.

"It's true. I nearly gave up hundreds of times. Your character was *much, much* better at coping." Richard handed me a clean hanky from his dressing-table. "You'll have to stop crying," he said, "otherwise I shall always be running out of handkerchiefs."

"Always?" I looked up at him.

"Yes, I want to be with you . . . when you cry, when you laugh. Always. . . Don't look like that. I mean it."

136

My thoughts were racing to the beat of my heart, as he held me very close and kissed me.

"Perhaps you'll feel different tomorrow when the gloss has worn off," I whispered, letting relief wash over my relaxing body as he held me.

It was a typical thing for me to say - to cover my emotions, as I'd been taught in the Army. It didn't put him off though. He lifted my face to meet his eyes. He grinned, then kissed me again very hard. When he stopped, we held each other close. I could feel his heart beating as quickly as mine.

"Oh, I wanted to do that ever since you stood crying in the Mall in all that rain." He kissed my eyelids. "But I thought I'd never get the chance. Everything kept going wrong. I never meant to hurt you."

"You didn't," I said. "I've just been hasty and stubborn, as usual. Are you sure you don't mind me being the way I am?"

"Pig-headed?" he joked, kissing me again. "I'll get used to it. I could get used to anything after walking around on sticks for months. Does that answer your question?" I knew what he meant.

"Yes," I answered quietly.

"Good." He grinned. "Now, wipe your eyes because, as soon as I've got myself tidied up, we're going to have the biggest private first night party ever."

"But it isn't the first night," I protested.

"It is for me. Because it's the first night *you* came to see me and . . ."

"And?"

Richard was smiling wickedly. "You'll find out."

"Why? Where are we going?" He was putting on his jacket.

"You'll see. I took the liberty of arranging something."

"What?"

"Dinner."

"Oh," I said. "But aren't you too tired?"

He laughed. "Come on."

* * *

"And this is your place?" I asked.

As I stood on the step outside he nodded and unlocked the door. I couldn't help thinking that all the stories I'd heard about poverty-stricken actors couldn't be true. He went in first and held open the door for me.

I turned from looking outside and said, "It's a lovely area."

"Yes, I was lucky to get the house at an excellent price. From a friend, who was going abroad."

I followed him along the deeply-carpeted pure white corridor. lined with modern pictures. Richard turned left into the lounge. It was white as well, cool, striking, the only splashes of colour in the red lampshades and the ornate wall hangings. It was ultra-modern. But the focal point of the room was a series of pictures with spotlights trained on them.

I went over and looked. "Why, they're all regiments!"

"Yes, another hobby of mine."

"They're very interesting."

I peered at them. Each one depicted soldiers in regimental dress, some dating back several hundred years.

Richard was watching me carefully. "Actually, they're family heirlooms. They belonged to my grandfather."

"You mean the one who was in the Gloucesters?"

"Correct. Anyway," he said, coming over to me, "don't let's waste any time. Come on." He took my hand and I followed him again through an adjoining door. It led into a beautiful small library. Once more, all white, the only colours being the spines of the books. "Mostly war, I'm afraid."

"Korean?"

"Correct. You were paying attention when I told you my life story at dinner last week."

"It's my training," I quipped. But my heart was thudding, because he was walking towards a curving oak banister. Were we going upstairs?

"You're not worried, are you?" It must have showed in my face.

"Course not," I said. "Why should I be?"

Why had I ever compared him to Martin? However, I was a little startled as we climbed up to the first floor: I could hear someone moving about.

He looked at me and grinned. "This house has three storeys," he explained. "We'll get there in the end."

"But who is that?" I asked.

"Come on." We turned off the deep-carpeted white landing into a much larger room. "My dining room."

The table was laid most beautifully with flowers, silver and napkins. And, to my amazement, there was a young man in black trousers, white shirt and bow tie opening a bottle of champagne. He smiled and continued. Dickon nodded to him affably.

"Gosh," I murmured.

At that moment, a smart middle-aged woman hurried out of what must have been the kitchen. "Good evening, Mr Maine. Good evening, madam."

"Good evening," I replied, shocked. Was Dickon rich enough to have servants?.

"Everything's prepared. The hot food's on the trolley. Shall I push it out for you?"

"No thank you, Elise," replied Dickon. "You can go now. We'll be absolutely fine."

"Excellent," she said. "Pedro?"

The dark-haired young man put the bottle in the bucket and carried it over to the table.

"Thanks," said Dickon.

"Oh, one thing, Mr Maine . . ." the woman was hesitating, "would you mind very much if I asked for your autograph? For my daughter. She's a fan of yours."

"Of course."

Next moment, the woman was withdrawing a small book and pencil. We waited while Dickon signed.

"Thanks so much. She'll be absolutely delighted. Well, goodnight, Mr Maine. Madam."

"Goodnight, sir. Madam," added Pedro.

With that, the two quickly let themselves out.

"Well," I said, impressed.

"Outside caterers, I'm afraid. Quite popular though. I may be making money out of this run, but not enough for servants."

"Thank goodness for that," I said. "I thought it was going to be like the Army with the orderlies standing watching while we ate."

He laughed and, taking me by the hand, led me to my place at table.

"I want to be alone with you," he said. My heart was racing. "And, the only way, was for someone else to do the cooking here. It's nicer than going to a restaurant, don't you think?"

"Much," I said truthfully. I was remembering how I'd felt in that Salisbury hotel; wishing I was with the right man. Now I was. . .

I remember thinking I would never forget that magical evening. First, the wonderful play and afterwards, the marvellous meal. We began with an exquisite starter, a fish mousse with artistic garnishing, followed by Dover Sole in a fantastic sauce. But the culmination of the meal was the sweet, bombe cassis, which melted in the mouth.

While Dickon was in the kitchen making the coffee, I walked over to the sash window, where the ivy curled round the frame. I looked out and breathed in the warm air. In fact, I felt very warm myself. Probably excitement

"You live in a lovely part of London," I called.

His long garden stretched down to the grounds of the Royal Hospital at Chelsea. I could smell roses but, in the distance, I thought I heard thunder.

"Yes. I have illustrious neighbours, too," he said, placing a silver tray on the table and coming to join me. "Nice old boys, the Chelsea Pensioners. They sit out there on their seats, and they're always ready with a story or two for anyone who wants to listen."

"Army again," I sighed.

"Afraid so. We can't get away from it, can we?"

"No."

"Never mind," said Dickon. "Come on."

"What about the washing up?" I asked, turning from the window.

"Oh, I'll shove that in the dishwasher."

"Where are we going?"

"For a better view. The penthouse." He grinned, picking up the tray with the coffee pot.

I followed him. . . "You are so lucky," I said, looking round.

"Please sit down."

I sank into a large burgundy leather armchair. Dickon's penthouse was a long room that stretched the length of the top storey, luxuriously-furnished with an expanse of windows. The colour scheme was deep reds and brown. It was very much a man's domain with its muted, masculine colours and prints, and looked well lived in.

On the whole, the penthouse was much more exotically furnished, richer than the sparse white of the living space on the bottom storey. I said so as he was pouring the coffee. He came over and handed me a cup. I sipped the fragrant liquid.

"Downstairs is my office really. It's the place where I meet people, etc. Not many visitors manage to get up here. I save it for special friends."

"I *am* lucky." I replied.

He held my gaze as he picked up his own coffee. To my embarrassment, I could feel my face getting hot.

I placed my cup on the small table beside me and, to cover my confusion, I strolled over to some patio doors, which seemed strange in a penthouse. I was delighted to see a pretty roof garden, full of roses and all the flowers that need the benefit of full sun, stretching into the circle of light thrown from the window.

"May I have a look?"

"Of course." Richard came over and unlocked the window, then pressed a hidden switch. Immediately the whole garden was floodlit. The effect was marvellous with lights hidden behind a profusion of flowering plants. And, somewhere, I could hear the noise of a fountain.

With Richard close behind me, I walked out into the fragrant night and drank in the air. But I could still hear far off thunder in this distance.

"This is magic," I said, walking along the crooked path towards the sound of the water. It was a tiny fountain, spurting from a horn of plenty carried by a white marble maiden. I stood there, enthralled. He was beside me now.

"A bit theatrical, do you think?"

"Oh, no, I love it. How *did* you find this lovely house?"

"I told you. I got it from a friend. A wealthy one. An American producer, actually." His eyes were twinkling now. "Success breeds success, you know."

"What do you mean?"

"Well, I've made a fair bit out of acting." He stood, staring at the fountain, then looked at me. "Did you know that a couple of years ago I used to be in a popular American soap?"

"No."

"Yes. I played a young and successful lawyer with a string of girlfriends. It hasn't been bought yet by an English TV company. Thank goodness."

"How fantastic!" I couldn't think of a thing to say.

"Not really. But the cheques were. Amazing . . . As for the girls . . ." he shrugged his shoulders, "I kept on looking for the right one."

"And you didn't find her?" My voice was wobbly.

"I did." Suddenly, Richard had his arms round me and I nestled my head against his shoulder.

"Who is she?" I wanted to hear him say it.

"Her name's Alison Dean, and she's with me now." I stayed silent. He brought up my head and cupped my face in his hands. "And I'm not shooting you a line. It's true. No amount of acting can make up for the real thing."

"I know." I smiled up at him. Then Dickon was kissing me, more seriously than he'd ever done. I opened my mouth under his and felt him sigh with delight. . . I wanted him so much. And all the unhappiness inside me was draining clean away. I had never known how wonderful it was to be in the right man's arms.

I don't know how long we stood there kissing but, all of a sudden, I felt an enormous drop of rain on my forehead; then we broke apart as a sliver of lightning sizzled across the orange glow of the city sky.

Richard and I ran back down the little path and, laughing, rushed through the patio doors into the dry. Then he was stroking my wet hair and kissing my forehead as the summer storm pounded outside. I realised that I hadn't taken any notice of my bad leg as I ran. It just felt so good to be there with him, to be warm and safe. I couldn't think of anything to say but, all at once, he was leading me over to another door at the end of the room, kissing me as we went.

"I think it's going to rain all night, Dickon," I said, watching him turn the handle.

"Good," he replied. "Then you won't be able to go home until after it's stopped, will you?"

Dickon's eyes were shining with love as he opened the door to the bedroom and gently pulled me through.

THE END

Also available in the

MYSTERIES OF THE HEART

Series

Forever Yours - Helen McCabe
The Sands of Time - Liberty Brett
Tides of Love - Helen McCabe

Peacock Publishing Ltd

Helen McCabe

Forever Yours

Lorne is working happily in Lanzarote, until her past,
in the shape of Shane Westonman shows up.
What was the intriguing secret she'd been hiding?

ISBN 0-9525404-8-7

Liberty Brett

THE SANDS OF TIME

What was the mystery surrounding Rik Fenton?
Pippa had to fly to Cairo to find out; a trip which led
her into deadly danger. But she was determined to
unravel the secret.

ISBN 0-9525404-3-6

Helen McCabe

Tides of Love

Could Fran's childhood sweetheart, Declan O'Neill, have been responsible for her father's mysterious death at sea?
One stormy night, Fran is prepared to risk everything to find out. Even her own life, and that of the man she loves.

ISBN 0-9525404-2-8

**Also available from Peacock Publishing Ltd
in the SPLENDOUR series**

Two for a Lie - Helen McCabe
Eve's Daughter - Michael Taylor
Raven's Mill - Helen McCabe

Forthcoming Title - Spring 1998

A Driving Passion - Michael Taylor

TWO FOR A LIE
Helen McCabe

'An epic saga blending historical fact, fiction and fantasy - a stunning read. I couldn't put it down!'
Susan Sallis

Mary Willcocks, aged eighteen, is returning home across the moor when she is waylaid and almost raped by the brutal Humphrey Moon, the wild young son of her former master. She is saved by her hero, Jem Farr, the half-French ward of the local squire. And Mary's love remains his throughout the many tragedies she has to face before her dreams come true.

Passion, intrigue, murder and revenge are the ingredients of this rich adventure set in the early 1800s. How Mary, the servant girl was transformed into the exotic PRINCESS CARABOO has puzzled scholars and her admirers for two hundred years. At last, her secrets are revealed in *Two for a Lie,* which is itself based on a dream as rich as Mary's own.

'*Two for a Lie* is more than a novel. Helen McCabe is a master storyteller with the unique gift of making history come alive in the astonishing adventures of her heroine. When I came away, I had a firsthand knowledge of early nineteenth-century life, and also found myself missing Mary . . .'
Shahrukh Husain

ISBN 0-9525404-0-1

Eve's Daughter

Michael Taylor

'A fascinating read. This highly enjoyable novel conveys vividly the flavour of life at the turn of the century.'
The Rt. Hon. Dr. John Gilbert, MP.

Lizzie Bishop, full of romantic dreams, finds fulfilment when she marries Ben Kite. But two former rivals for her affection, Stanley Dando, her enigmatic second cousin, and Jesse Clancey, the likeable and handsome son of a prosperous neighbour, remain secretly in love with her. Then Ben, with the noblest of intentions, makes the biggest mistake of his life, and everybody is caught up in the spiralling consequences.

Sensual, riveting, poignantly tender, and often hilariously funny, Eve's Daughter draws the reader into an enthralling saga of obsessive desire and deceit. Set in a Black Country community in the early 20th century, the characters are engaging and vividly true to life. A brilliant debut novel.

'Michael Taylor comes into that small group of male writers able to achieve a warm empathy with the heroine.'
Dr. Hilary Johnson.

'From the first sentence it grips your attention . . . an absorbing read.'
Leigh Rowley - The Dudley News

ISBN 0-9525404-5-2

RAVEN'S MILL

Helen McCabe

'Helen McCabe has done it again! Well researched; believable characters and a chillingly realistic villain.'
Sue Sallis.

Beautiful Lydia Annesley returns to Upwych from London at the age of eighteen to take her rightful place as heiress to a salt fortune. To her dismay, she discovers that handsome, brooding Caleb Vyne, who is both her business rival and the master of sinister Raven's Mill, appears to have other ideas. Lydia soon finds out to her cost, what price she has to pay for her beauty, her fortune, and her business.

This tender and passionate love story, set against an authentic background of the Victorian salt industry, draws the reader into the world of powerful brinemasters grappling for total supremacy. But feisty heroine, Lydia Annesley, can hold her own in both love and the salt business. The unusual background for this novel makes for both an exciting and rewarding read.

'. . . a terrific novel. I enjoyed its dramatic intensity and the historical backdrop very much. . .'
Victoria Evans, Carlton UK

ISBN 0-9525404-1-X

A Driving Passion

Michael Taylor

Lovely Henzey Kite is wary of allowing herself to fall in love
again after her first heady affair with prosperous man-about-
town, Billy Witts. But men find her beauty and her talent as
an artist irresistible. Then, deeply drawn to handsome engi-
neer Will Parish, a widower, Henzey finds another man vying
for her love; wealthy motor manufacturer Dudley Worthington,
a married man. Only Dudley is aware of the astonishing links
between these three men; links that are enough to turn all
their lives upside-down. . .

Set within the external glamour and internal graft of the
burgeoning West Midlands' motor industry in the 20s and 30s,
A Driving Passion is a spellbinding saga of obsession, agonising
love and restless guilt.

A sequel to *Eve's Daughter*, this compulsive tale confirms
Michael Taylor as one of the few male writers able to achieve
a warm empathy with the heroine.

Due out Spring 1998

ISBN 0-9525404-6-0

All Peacock books are available at your local bookshop. In case of difficulty, they can be obtained from:

Littlehampton Book Services Ltd.,
10-14 Eldon Way
Lineside Industrial Estate
Littlehampton
West Sussex BN17 7HE
United Kingdom

Direct Sales Line:
01903 736736 (fax no. 01903 730828)
International +44 1903 736736 (International fax +44 1903 730828)
Please quote the title you require, author, ISBN, and credit card number - Visa/MasterCard.

Card No. _____

Expiry Date _____

Signature _____

Peacock Publishing Ltd. reserves the right to charge new retail prices, if necessary, which may differ from those shown.

Address to which book(s) to be forwarded: Quantity _____

Name _____

Address_____

_____

Please allow 28 days for delivery